Smokescreen

Ewan Lawrie

Copyright ©2022 By Ewan Lawrie

All rights reserved.

No portion of this book may be reproduced in any form without written permission from the publisher or author, except as permitted by U.S. copyright law.

Foreword

This book was written in 2007, to meet the Nanowrimo challenge that year. After a few months work I published it at Bubok.com. Thankfully, it is no longer available, as it had the worst typesetting I've ever seen. No-one to blame but me for that, however.

Anyway, see where I got "the future" wrong and where I got it right. I think it stands up. I love D.I. Murray. Maybe you will too.

Chapter 1

Nom-de-fume

It was a stupid game. But we were going to play it anyway.

'Voodoo Chile.' It came out sharply; a challenge.

'Hendrix.' He gave a rapid reply. Both of us had played it all our working lives.

'All Along the Watchtower.' I said. Second and last musical association.

The game often turned on the next go: the first completely random one.

'Jehovah's Witnesses.'

Harry smirked. Rubbed a forefinger and thumb together, drained the last of his Guinness with port depth-charge.

'Amish!' I shouted.

Harry turned white. I busked a rendition of a long defunct game-show's time-out tune, counted down from 5 to zero in my head. Harry turned sulkily and went to the bar. It was a short game, for us. You only got a five count. If you came up with nothing, you bought the drinks. The game was played by bored people all over the country; in canteens, clubs and bars. We were in a blokey, smoky bar. Not licensed premises, of course. A private bar. A downstairs, backstreet Soho bar. No King's Head, Blacksmith's Arms, Farter's Arse hanging from a yardarm outside. So you could smoke. And everyone did. No dope, though. Carlton Woodbine wouldn't have that; it was his bar after all. We called the place No 6, because it was. Number six I mean. Carlton was black. No-one was brave enough to ask if it was his real name. Must of us went by a nom-de-fume. Now that smoking had been driven underground.

Harry came back with two highball glasses sporting parasols and parrot feathers.

'What's that you cunt?'

'Blue Lightning.'

'What's in it?'

'I don't know, just drink it, Ray.'

I took a sip. Then a draw on a Marlboro. Harry was smoking Luckies.

'I've heard rumours of Embassy available at Vauxhall, Ray.'

'Get off, how? The last factory closed in January.'

'There was a raid on a Bond Warehouse. Someone had forgotten about 2 million cigarettes.They've been there since... well, since prohibition started.'

'Which gang? Plato's?'

'Dunno. Who cares?'

'Must have been a tip-off!' I laughed.

I hadn't had an English cigarette in two years. No-one had. Vauxhall would be busy.

'What's the craic? '

'We interested?'

'Course we are; the Met's finest aren't we? I think we need to make sure these cigarettes don't fall into the wrong hands.'

'Midnight. At the Bridge. That's all I know.'

'Drink up, Harry. We'll call by the office, make sure no-one else has got wind of it.'

'Customs and Excise, you mean?'

'Them too.' We waved at Carlton Woodbine, who didn't wave back.

11.30. We were parked in sight of Vauxhall Bridge. No mean feat. Of course the £500 congestion charge meant there was plenty of room on the road-side. It was just that there wasn't often a gap between the mounds of uncollected refuse. A rat stopped half-way across the bonnet, looked in at Harry and I.

'Kindred spirits,' I said.

'We could be on other spirits instead of this wild-goose chase, Ray.'

'God, I need a fag.'

'Well, you should be able to pick up a few soon.'

'You know what I mean.'

'Ray, how many times? This is our place of work. What if Joe Public sees us lighting up?' He passed me his second-to-last Lucky.

'Joe Public won't be out. Curfew breakers are criminals. We are the Law.'

We both cracked up laughing, coughing the first draw-ful of smoke out.

An olive green pantechnicon pulled to a halt on the Westminster end. Harry pulled out a pair of binos.

'Driver and mate. No hardware. Tailgate's down. Fuckin' hell!'

'What?'

'Like roaches. Bout a hundred, where did they come from? Did you see them?'

'Any faces?'

'Can't tell from here, these binos aren't much cop.'

'Neither are you. Let's go and throw our weight about. Get the pump-action out of the boot.'

The first ten customers had taken their snout and melted away, by the time we reached the giant lorry. The driver and mate were in combat dress. Not a gang then. A bit of business on the side for the Army. You couldn't blame them, according to the Internet they hadn't been paid in six months. That kind of story wasn't on the BBC. And you couldn't get a satellite signal, not since Menwith Hill had switched the jumbo jammer on. ITV, of course, didn't show any news at all. One good thing about being a copper, at least we could get access to the Internet. Joe Public hadn't had broadband access since the pictures of the Foreign Secretary with a transsexual prostitute in India had appeared. They said the pictures were faked, naturally. But they weren't. You could check that out with off-the-shelf software. Or you could then.

The driver nodded at us:

'Bill?'

'Yeah.' We chorused.

'Is it how much or how many?'

'We'll take cigs.'

'How many?'

'How many do you have?

'200,000 or so.'

'We'll take half.'

'And where will you put that many?'

'We won't, you'll get a police escort out of the capital via our nick.'

The soldier grunted. His mate said:

'Can we sell the rest first? You'll hang around? Shouldn't take more than an hour.'

'Give us twenty on account.' I said.

'Yeah, on account I haven't had an Embassy in 2 years.' Harry sniggered.

'Here, kill yourselves.' The soldier said and tossed us a 200 carton.

The queue was down to two. A tallish guy came running from the Westminster side, long coat flapping behind him. Cashmere. I nudged Harry. Nodded at the latecomer. Harry looked, smiled. It was Christmas. It was the Home Secretary. We waited; his turn came. He took 2000, ten cartons. He took in our faces and the warrant cards held up beside them. Exhaling he said:

'It's not how it looks.'

'But I think it is.' I said.

'Look, you obviously know who I am... I can-'

'You can't.' Harry cut him off. 'Mr Home Secretary, I am arresting you..'

'Do you really need to hear that? You must have signed it off.' My turn to interrupt.

'Do you read everything you sign, officer?' He seemed unfazed.

'It's Detective Inspector, sir. And yes I do, always.'

He gave the brilliant, vote-winning smile that had gained a Scot a Home Counties seat:

'Of course, well OK, we'll assume I know my rights, such as they are.'

I turned to Harry; told him to get the soldiers' details from their ID cards and get rid of them, but not before getting us some more evidence to smoke later.

'Worth risking everything for a cigarette, is it, sir?'

I wanted to needle him, get past the invulnerability of the politician.

'You know how it is... I bet you've been dying for a fag yourself, hmm?'

The cultured Morningside tones and the raised eyebrow did it. I smashed him in the gut with my fist. Harry looked away.

'Let's get him in the car, Harry. See how he feels down at the station, I think he's got stomach trouble.'

'I didn't know the PM smoked, did you?' Harry wanted to know.

'I don't even know if my wife does, and she's about as likely to turn up in Number Six as the Prime Minister.'

'Speaking of which, you going home tonight?'

'No, won't make it before lights out. I'm going to doss here, one of the cells.'

'You don't mind if I take the works vehicle? I'll blues and twos the last few miles. I'll get most of the way... before.'

'Keep the shotgun in the front with you. Be careful out there.'

We sniggered: before satellite went we used to laugh at the repeats of old cop shows, especially the Yank ones. Rumour had it Sat TV would have gone in 2010 if it hadn't been for the Olympics. In the end it made no difference: the Yanks getting their arse kicked in Iran was the spectator sport of choice in 2012. And London and the UK was flat broke as a consequence. I waved Harry off. Went back to interview room 3, switched the tape to play. Something bothered me about the interview. I listened to it 3 or 4 times. No, it wouldn't come. I put the tape in my pocket.

Out front Jerry Patel was still ignoring his book, the one he had been so interested in, before.

'Hey, Jerry. Quiet night, eh?'

'It was... That was-'

'Yes, it was. You'll never guess. Some army blokes were flogging fags over at Vauxhall Bridge. Chummy came running up and joined the queue for ciggies. We just pulled him in for the fun of it. I wacked him one you know.'

'I can think of a few of them I'd want to lump.' He allowed.

'Yeah well... Listen Jerry, Mum's the word, right?'

He looked doubtful.

'I'll put a word in with Elvis – about CID, how about that?'

He gave a crisp nod and grunted 'OK.'

Job done. I went off to cell number 3 for a kip. It was my lucky number: so I slept.

Chapter 2

"Do they have bike sheds there?"

I drove. Harry sat with the Honourable Member for Chichester West in the back. Around 70 per cent of the street-lighting was working and would continue to do so until 3 a.m. After that the power to the
city went off until 8 in the morning. The government said it was part of its overall ecology strategy. It was an effort to make demand meet the supply. We were lucky in London. In Oxford, Edinburgh and Cardiff the power had been off since 11 p.m.

'Always smoked, sir?'

'Since Fettes.'

I laughed: 'Do they have bike sheds there? That's where I smoked: at Maryhill Comp.'

'England and the English, Inspector: nothing without the Scots, are they?'

'Nothing much with them now, sir, are they?'

He bit his lip, coloured a little:

'And that's why-' but he stopped. He'd not had to appear on Newsnight for years: I wondered what Paxman and the like were doing now.

Harry let out a snore as we pulled into the station car park. He woke with a jolt, blinked a few times. We all got out of the car. The Home Secretary appeared to be looking round for photographers. I put my arm through his and dragged him up the steps.

Jerry Patel was on the desk. He was reading a novel. The Impressionist or something, it was called. Didn't know he was interested in art.

'Jerry! Interview room 3 free?'

'Yeah, shall I book him in n-.' He broke off when he looked up from the book and clocked who we had.

'No, just get on with your reading, hey.' But he turned the book over and began shaking his head slowly.

I sat the politician in the chair, told Harry to stand by the door. I walked over to the 3 drawer metal filing cabinet in the corner. Picked up an old twin deck cassette recorder. Checked it was loaded. Amazingly it was. I started a sneezing fit from the dust disturbed when I moved it. The player sat on the table, for a few moments the for a few moments the tired spindles whirr was the only sound in the room.

'Memory Lane sir, hey? Before PACE Code X. This is the last tape recorder in the building you know. Still, you know the tape's not for your protection, don't you? The prisoner will identify himself for the tape.'

He said nothing. Harry gave him a slap on the back of the head.

'Ah well, some of Code X applies at least...' I observed.

The voice was shaky as he gave the name at last: that gave me some satisfaction.

'Did you buy an illegal substance - that is tobacco - tonight sir?'

'You know the answer to that.'

'Don't hit him so hard, Harry. They'll hear it on the tape.'

I laughed. Nobody would ever hear it, if I could help it.

'Just answer yes or no, sir.'

'Yes, yes I did.'

'And how many cigarettes was it sir?'

'2000.'

'Were they for personal use?'

'Of course... Of course they were.'

'That's quite a lot of cigarettes. I'm on 10 a day. That's a lot nowadays. That's nearly 9 months supply for me, isn't it, Harry?'

Harry laughed: 'It would be unless you count all the ones you smoke of mine.'

'You see, sir, I just don't think they were all for you. That means possession with intent to sell. That's not a cautionable, sir.'

He was silent.

'Well were they?'

'I wasn't aware you'd asked a question, Inspector.'

'Were the fags just for you or not?' I spat.

'No,' he said. 'They were for the PM, all of them. I don't smoke now myself.'

Harry spat on the floor: 'Fucking great!' he said.

The minister looked surprised at his own admission.

'Late night sitting was it, in the House?' I asked him.

'I was in the House of Commons bar, with the PM.'

'Won't he be waiting for you?'

'No, I don't think he will.' He smiled, more twitched a mouth corner, really.

'Interview terminated at 02.30 17 April 2013.' I clicked the recorder off.

'You didn't signal the start of the interview, Inspector.' Some of the sang-froid had returned.

'No, I don't believe I did. Doesn't take long to forget how it's done, does it?'

'What?'

'Any number of things, police work, justice, civil liberty... you choose.'

He had the grace not to reply. We took him out front. Jerry must have been in the bog. The custody desk wasn't manned. Naughty.

'You have about 25 minutes before the lights go out, Minister. Best get moving.'

'Better had.'

He strode out of the station yard as if he owned the city. Perhaps he did.

'I didn't know the PM smoked, did you?' Harry wanted to know.

'I don't even know if my wife does, and she's about as likely to turn up in Number Six as the Prime Minister.'

'Speaking of which, you going home tonight?'

'No, won't make it before lights out. I'm going to doss here, one of the cells.'

'You don't mind if I take the works vehicle? I'll blues and twos the last few miles. I'll get most of the way... before.'

'Keep the shotgun in the front with you. Be careful out there.'

We sniggered: before satellite went we used to laugh at the repeats of old cop shows, especially the Yank ones. Rumour had it Sat TV would have gone in 2010 if it hadn't been for the Olympics. In the end it made no difference: the Yanks getting their arse kicked in Iran was the spectator sport of choice in 2012. And London and the UK was flat broke as a consequence. I waved Harry off. Went back to interview room 3, switched the tape to play. Something bothered me about the interview. I listened to it 3 or 4 times. No, it wouldn't come. I put the tape in my pocket.

Out front Jerry Patel was still ignoring his book, the one he had been so interested in, before.

'Hey, Jerry. Quiet night, eh?'

'It was... That was-'

'Yes, it was. You'll never guess. Some army blokes were flogging fags over at Vauxhall Bridge. Chummy came running up and joined the queue for ciggies. We just pulled him in for the fun of it. I wacked him one you know.'

'I can think of a few of them I'd want to lump.' He allowed.

'Yeah well... Listen Jerry, Mum's the word, right?'

Chapter 3

'The Pound is at 40 cents on the Euro this morning'

There was a quiet knocking on the open cell door. It was Sergeant Patel: with a mug of tea in his hand.

'How the fuck did you do that?'

'I bring a camping stove in: got to have a cuppa, Gov.'

'Bet the Health and Safety Nazis don't know about that. That would be a four pager.'

'Yeah... I take it out before 8, that's why you're getting it now. Four pager? You're havin' a laugh. That twat Smithson's last risk assessment kept these cells in toilet paper for a week!'

'Thanks, Jerry.'

Maybe I would put in a word, at that. I looked at my watch; it was 0715. 45 minutes to power. The Assistant Chief Constable; David 'Elvis' Pressley, wouldn't be in until half eight. If Harry pitched up before then, too bad. Those are the breaks, Jerry, I thought. Nice tea, though.

Harry came in at about 8.15. I was in the canteen. The TVs were on. One in each corner, all tuned to the single BBC channel. They did well to be able to start programming as the power came on. News: grey men telling us what the government wanted us to know. I'd have thought the presenters were CGI if I'd believed for one minute the BBC could afford such things. Harry sat opposite me. The station was full now: uniforms, WPCs too: since the power situation began, the Federation had insisted it was unsafe for them to work after lights out. No night shifts. I took a deep sniff of the air:

'Smell that, Harry!'

'What? I can't smell anything.'

He looked around, hunting for the source of the non-existent smell.

'Exactly,' I said. 'Remember the smell of the frying food... the cigarette smoke?'

'Don't be daft, Ray. I joined the Force in 2003. Of course I don't remember the smoke. What I wouldn't give for a full English though, eh?'

'Yeah...'

The financial bit came on.

'The Pound is at 40 cents on the Euro this morning, slightly up in expectation of the PM's speech in the house today. The FTSE broke the 2000 mark for the first time in 2 years today, fuelled by rumours that the PM has a startling announcement on rejoining the EU....'

I tuned it out. We'd rejoin or we wouldn't. But the electorate would have little or no control over the matter. I asked Harry:

'Got any Euros?'

'Yeah, some... pulled a Spanish diplomat in Soho. Arguing over the bill. Didn't realize that a smoke afterwards was extra. I split his cash with Demetrios.'

'What, your brother did that willingly, then?'

'What do you think? His club'd have been shut long ago, without me.'

'When did you lift someone last, Harry?' I cocked my head.

'Nick or send down, for jail time, like?'

'A real bang-to-rights, minimum of 10 years, take him down,collar?'

'Dunno... coupla years?'

'What for?'

'Paedo. Musician.'

'Gary Glitter.' I paused. 'Gotcha! One... two...

A voice came from over my shoulder:

'Max Headroom.'

'Not a musician...' I turned to look at the voice's owner.

'Fraid so. Released a single '82 '83 - something like that.'

The ACC, 'Elvis' Pressley grinned. I had a dim memory of a TV programme, when I was 10... something apocalyptic in the title.

'But he wasn't a real person....Sir!'

'Who is?' he said. 'My office, now. Both of you.'

Elvis' office was on the top floor. A view of the high-rises and smog at our end of town. Could have been the view from any borough, except for theme-park London; the West End, Canary Wharf, Westminster. The City and the Country spent some money there, in the hope of attracting some Euros, now the dollars never came. A good TV was in the corner. Sport now: Chelsea had qualified for UEFA. First British club in Europe for a long, long time. The players were all English now.

The super-rich mercenaries had long gone: when the Russian Oligarchs had taken their money to safer havens. Zurich Grasshoppers had won the Champions League 3 times in the last 5
years.

'Sit down, gentlemen.'

We sat, we waited. Elvis flicked through a pair of very thick personnel files. I didn't need to guess whose.

'Umm, you're probably wondering why I've called you in - nothing to worry about, exactly. Just... Anything you'd like to tell me?'

I saw Harry start to open his mouth, a discreet but hard kick silenced him.

'No... I don't think so, sir.'

He gave us both a hard look, the avuncular, diffident manner had disappeared.

'You'd better be very sure about that.'

Elvis stood up. Hands behind the back, the Royal position we called it. Important people walk about like this: it stops them doing inappropriate things with their hands – like putting them in pockets, or smoking a cigarette.

'Look at this.' He indicated one of the 20-or-so photos on his vanity wall.

The picture was old. Elvis looked about 30, no uniform. From the car in the background it looked to be about '93, the year I'd joined the Met. It was just him and some suits, outside a building. The ACC didn't wait for any reaction, just pointed at another picture:

'And this.'

Elvis again, more than 10 years later. Most of the suits were the same people. There was a uniformed copper in the photo. Lots of scrambled egg on the hat.

'Gregory Peck, that one, isn't it?' I pointed at the hat.

'Star of the Boys from Brazil? God he hated that nickname. You'll notice he's not in this photograph?'

He'd moved on to the most recent photograph. 8 of the 10 in this one had been in the original, including Elvis and the man Harry and I had had in the interview room last night.

'Sit down, there's going to be something interesting on in a minute.'

We swivelled our chairs to look up at the TV in the corner.

'The scheduled broadcast by the Prime Minister has been cancelled.'

The grey man on the screen was almost showing some animation.

'We're going live to Number 10 for a statement from a cabinet office spokesman.'

A man with a piece of paper stood in front of the familiar door with no handle. There were a few microphones in front of him. I wondered which countries this broadcast would actually reach.

'The Prime Minister was found dead this morning in the Palace of Westminster. A Police Investigation is underway to determine the cause of death. Jackie Carlton, the Foreign Minister will make a further statement in the House today. The British Public are requested to remain calm and we emphasise that it is 'business as usual, for the time being.'

Elvis clicked the remote. Looked hard at us. I stared back. Harry suddenly found the depressing view fascinating 'You know what's expected, Murray?'

I gave a respectful grunt. He nodded at me; 'I hope so, at least. That's all.'

And he began flicking through the files again, not seeing a word. Bad luck, Jerry, I thought.

Harry and I were in the car. Driving aimlessly. It was about 10 a.m.

'Let's have one then.'

'Have what, Ray?'

'A fry-up, Full English.'

'Shaftesbury? You can't park there, Ray. Not without a dip plate or a tourist's rental car.'

'Fuck off, Harry. We're the law, I wish you'd remember that.'

He didn't look happy, but he flicked the indicator just the same.

Shaftesbury Avenue itself was all that was left of Theatreland. The businesses in between theatres sold Theme Park Britain to the Spanish, New European and Japanese tourists. So you had fish-and-chip restaurants, haggis shops and all day full fry,heart-attack-on-a-plate cafés alongside shops selling fake or real Burberry, Water Biscuits and Barbours. That kind of food was taxed beyond the spending power of the rest of Britain. Harry and I would need a good few of his Euros to get our fix of lard.

He pulled in beside a parking meter, yanked a placard saying police out of the glove box and slapped it on the dashboard. We entered the Sunshine Café in silence.

The waitress turned up. Marina Zipowicz on a badge on her black-and-white uniform; one of the Poles stranded here when the border closed and we reneged on the Schengen.

'Euros first.' Pad and pencil still in one hand by her side.

Harry pulled out a thick roll. Marina's face lit up.

'Do you want a room in the back?'

We both said yes at the same time. A chance for Nicotine. The waitress's gait had modified somewhat since she'd seen the money. Straighter, with a sway.

'Full English? Do you need extras?' She licked her lips.

'Yes, two, and no we have our own.'

Harry held up a packet of Embassy – and Marina's eyes glittered. The sway reached comedy proportions.

The food came.

'What's up, Harry?'

'That stuff, last night.'

'What about it?'

'You fucking walloped the second highest-ranking member of the government, that's what!'

'Oh that. Interesting, don't you think?'

Harry looked at me, searched my face for a clue, fork with a glistening piece of sausage suspended before his mouth.

'Why?' he said. The sausage disappeared, left a trail of grease on his chin.

'I wonder what the time of death is on the PM?' I said.

Harry started to choke. I got up whacked him hard between the shoulder blades. Twice. The offending sausage landed on my plate. I'd lost my appetite anyway. Harry looked like he'd trod in dog-shit on his way to meet the King.

'Oh, for fuck's sake.' was all he said.

I slipped the Polish waitress a ten euro note that I'd bummed off Harry. She slipped me her phone number on a scrap of paper torn from her pad. Quid pro quo.

'Number Six?' I asked.

'Are we going to do any policing today?' Harry wanted to know.

'Business as usual, I think the Government mouthpiece said.'

'Fair enough, let's go see if we can get a smile out of Mr Woodbine.'

Harry smiled. Relieved. We accelerated away from the Sunshine Café into the drizzle.

Chapter 4

Details Don't Matter

The Number Six was almost deserted. Woodbine was polishing a glass, a roll-your-own stuck to his bottom lip. Not a papiros: it was real cigarette paper, not newspaper or Izal toilet roll. We paid plenty for the drinks in the Number Six.

'Harry, Ray.' A nod: talkative for Woodbine.

'Woodbine.2 Guinness and whatever Ray's having.'

A lip-twitch, not quite a laugh: a tiny victory in the war against Woodbine's inscrutability.

I wiped the bitter froth from my upper-lip. Harry used his lizard tongue to clean his.

'Stick the telly on, Woodbine.'

'What for?' he said.

'Heard the news? The PM.'

'Oh him. What's the diff, eh? There'll be another one along, I ain't voted since '97.'

'Shame on you.'

I wagged a finger at him. The twitch came again. Last year's election was the first time the Met had been called on to 'escort' voters to the booths. 85 % turn out in the Metropolitan area: the experiment would spread to the rest of England, next time. Didn't matter, there was only the Tony Party to vote for.

Woodbine zapped the remote.

'And now to Downing Street for a statement from the Foreign Secretary...'

'Jackie' Carlton appeared. Pinstripe tailored suit. Late 40's, well preserved. I found her sexy. Liked the aura of authority she wore so easily. The North-East accent was a turn-on too. Born in Ashington, some Central Office wag had dubbed her Jackie after Blair had asked her if she was related to the footballing brothers. It stuck: didn't hold her back. Maybe Blair had been right, details don't matter.

'As you may know, the PM is no longer with us. Circumstances of his death are unclear, but the Cabinet Office are being kept abreast of events by Assistant Chief Constable Pressley of the Metropolitan Police, Head of a specially constituted Task For-'

I missed the next few seconds. Harry looked like a ghost. Woodbine raised his eyebrows:

'Another drink?'

'Long Island Iced Tea.' Harry was fucking weird.

'Whiskey, Woodbine. Double.' I said.

Carlton was taking questions from pet reporters now.

'Foreign Minister, can you explain why you are pro tem leader of the government when the constitution clearly calls for the Home Sec-'

'There are special circumstances which we are unable to reveal at this time.'

She seemed to be looking behind the camera for... What? Encouragement, confirmation... clues?

'Minister, is there any truth in the rumour that Martial Law is about to be declared?'

'The Cabinet Office have been in discussion with the Chiefs-Of-Staff, yes, but no decision has been made at this time.'

'One more thing-'

A suited lackey stepped forward,

'That's all. No more questions at this time.'

He escorted the Minister out of shot.

'Ray.' Harry looked at me like a Bloodhound at the vet's.

'What?'

'I'm going back to the station and I'm putting in a leave pass. Or I'm going sick. I've got kids.'

I exhaled. Savoured the Guinness and whiskey breath.

'Yeah... you do that. I'll drop you off.'

'What about you?'

'My kid doesn't like me.' I said.

Harry waved on his way out of the station yard. I hoped the tube was running far enough out for him today. I ran up the station steps. The sergeant on the desk was Gina. Gina Douglas. Everyone called her Gina Gina.

'Gina G...Sarge. Anything for me?' I said, praying for a no.

'The Super, the Super's looking for you. Looking for you.'

'Yeah...I'll call his office.' I waggled my mobile at her.

'He said straight to him. Straight to his office he said.'

'You could say you hadn't seen me?'

'I could, Inspector, yes I could.'

A meaty hand slapped on the desk. 'But ye won't, so ye won't!'

Gina was stunned beyond all repetition. I followed the arm up the uniform sleeve towards the silvered symbols on the epaulette. Above the thick neck was the blocky and ever-reddened face of Superintendent Doug McCracken. McCrackers was his inevitable nickname. Always angry, prone to prolonged and colourful outbursts of swearing, everyone in the Station was terrified of him. Me included.

'Sir, I was just going..'

'No you weren't, you fucking lying Prod.'

I braced myself for a flood of obscenities. They didn't come.

'Right, my office now.'

I followed meekly up the fire exit stairs. The lift was out of order, again. McCrackers was causing sparks with the metal in his heels. Maybe a fire would start and I'd escape.

The Super's office was on the same floor as the ACC's. Smaller, dirtier and more impersonal than Elvis's, it was more intimidating all the same. A postage-stamp window's view was obscured by a Venetian blind that hadn't moved in a decade. A pull on the string and every blade would have cascaded to the grubby lino floor. I sat in the plastic and tubular steel chair opposite McCrackers. He steepled his fingers, breathed in deeply; maybe 10 breaths.

'Anger management. Valuable tool.'

'Yessir.'

He glared at me over the steeple. A wrathful God eying the Godless outside his church.

'Don't take the piss out of me. Inspector Murray. You Hun scum are all the same.'

'I support St Johnstone, sir.'

'Even worse! Ye won't even tayek saides. Yer not whyze.'

McCracker's Belfast bollocks got stronger and stronger the angrier he got. I wondered how to defuse the situation.

'What's this about, sir?'

'That fucking politician!'

'I can explain...'

'What the fuck are you on about? What have you got to do with the ACC swanning off to Westminster on a special Task Force? Are you in charge of the Met now? You scunner! Are ye takin' the piss?'

He loomed over the desk. No wonder the Irish Rugby Union had sent a *letter* to tell him he wouldn't be representing his country. There'd been an unfortunate incident in the Met versus Combined Services match in 1991.

'Nothing, sir. Nothing.' Maybe the Super had caused Gina's verbal tic.

'Anyway, Pressley's asked for a DI. I'm sending you. You'll tell me what's going on, that smarmy bastard. He's a fockin' creep, I tell ye. Even at Hendon. He knows fockin' nothin' aboyt polace work.'

He swept his in- and out-trays off the desk. I realised why the furniture was so cheap in his office.

'Right sir, Right. I'll be going. Where is the Operations Room for the Task Force?'

He started to laugh. Looked almost human.

'Ye'll like it fine. They've set up in the House Of Commons Bar.'

That was my cue. I left.

It looked like you'd imagine it. Dark wood panelling, brass fittings on the bar. Portraits of long-dead politicians on the walls. Tables had been shoved together. Laptops were connected up in an impromptu network. The ACC was sitting on one of the velvet covered banquettes in conversation with a suit. Not a good suit. Civil - or Secret - Service I guessed. There were about 3 uniforms excluding Elvis's: 5 CID including me. A pretty pathetic Task Force. I stood at the bar waiting to come into Pressley's eye-line. The bar wasn't open. Pity.

'Murray! Here.'

He patted the velvet beside him. Back to avuncular. You couldn't trust some 'Uncles' though, could you?

'Sit, sit.' He was almost jovial.

'What is it then? A murder, suicide, act of God, what?'

'Oh, it's foul play alright.'

'All sewn up already, sir?'

He smiled, I wondered about his Uncle act again. 'You might say that,' he said.

'What do I do, then?'

'I knew he'd send you, you know.'

He rubbed his hands down his cheeks, shook his head, as if to clear his ears, mind - or even conscience.

'I'm counting on you to know what to do, when it's time. Meanwhile, get the bar open. Enjoy yourself.'

'But, sir, what about the investigation?'

'It will be satisfactorily concluded, don't worry.'

I half expected him to rub a finger along the side of his nose.

'So what do I do?'

'You'll do what you normally do, I imagine.'

I turned to the barman who'd appeared behind the gleaming brass pump.

'Give me a half.'

'What would sir like? We have Guinness, Old Peculier -very popular with the members- German Lager, French, Belgian...?'

'One of everything, give me one of everything. It's going to be a very long day.'

My mobile beeped. An SMS. Obviously not urgent. The Short Message Service could deliver in seconds, hours or even weeks. Coverage dropped out, messages queued for days, servers went down and looters took down the masts in the dead of night to sell the metal for scrap. Police officers carried mobiles because it was procedure, a relic from when things like that actually worked as advertised. I thumbed the buttons. Harry Xeno's number.

'12.00.Get to a TV.'

It was 11.55. I snapped at the Barman to turn the TV on. He looked blank.

'Go on, I know you've got one under the counter, for when it's slow.'

It was a guess, but a good one.

'In a few moments we'll be going live to the nerve centre of the Police Task Force investigating the PM's sudden death. We have news of a high-profile arrest'

There was a commotion, Kilgour, the Home Secretary came in, a uniform either side of him. The press were behind, TV and print. Kilgour was grinning.

'And now live to Task Force Central in Westminster...

A TV reporter in front of the Palace of Westminster started up in that earnest, pompous voice they save for disasters and world exclusives.

'In a dramatic development in the investigation the Home Secretary has today been called in to the Task Force HQ to help the Police with their enquiries...'

The TV switched to a shot of a marked car arriving. Kilgour was frog-marched into the building. The BBC as usual were pretending everything was live: they cut to the reporter.

'A police spokesman has declined to comment...'

I looked over at Kilgour. He and Elvis were chatting over on the velvet.

The press having turned up were huddled just inside the door, not sure what to do. A few looked impatient; old enough to remember what a D-notice was, but the majority were just waiting for someone in government to tell them what to report. 'Needles' Sharpe from the Standard was chewing a biro. I waved him over.

'Drink, Needles?' I pointed at my row of half-pints.

'Don't mind if I do? Cheers, Ray.'

He necked the Guinness in a oner, smacked his lips.

'Fuckin' lovely. Even better when the Bill pays.'

'This one's on the Government, Needles.'

'Shit, We'll pay for it sooner or later, then.'

'I was just thinking the same myself.'

Needles nickname wasn't just down to his surname. Earlier in his career, he had been noted for always getting the Politicos to say the wrong thing, needling them until the mask slipped and they said something they might actually believe. MPs would see him in the Press Gallery and find a reason to talk to the Guardian or the Independent – or even Woman's Own. He didn't look so scary: stood about 5'5". His shirt was hanging out, a denim Jacket was mis-buttoned about half-way up and there was a dark patch on the front of his chinos. I liked him; there was still enough of the reporter in him to make him worth talking to.

'What do you know, Needles?'

I ushered him further towards the corner of the bar, pushing half pint glasses along the surface.

'I know not to trust the filth.' He smiled, showing crooked, stained teeth.

'Not even a fellow smoker?' I asked.

'Especially them.'

'Thing is... I'm not sure what I know either.'

'Want to talk about it?' The teeth appeared again.

'Yeah, only... confidential. Could be an exclusive in it for you.'

He started a laughing fit then... it bubbled out of him, he couldn't contain it. He laughed like a man who hadn't laughed in half a lifetime. Perhaps he hadn't. He got control of himself:

'Just who would print it, eh?'

'I don't know. One of the European dailies?'

'It would have to be a hell of a story, wouldn't it? I mean, if it's about this lot, I couldn't come back, could I?'

'Can't talk here, Needles. Eleven, tonight. Slug and Lettuce, Canary Wharf, bring some Euros. Or put me on expenses.'

The laughing started once more: even harder, as if he was frightened he never would again.

Chapter 5

'Does a tree fall in the wood?'

Twenty minutes later, Needles is gone. I'm alone except for five empties and the last half. It's cider: I've left it 'til last, it's the street-alkie's drink of choice and I've never liked it much. I'm in the 2-pint buzz-zone. Everything feels right; you know the next thing out of your mouth will be witty, insightful or both. A hardened drinker can make this feeling last a long time, as long as 8 or 9 pints. Like every drinker, I know that after that it'll end in puke and punches. I can handle it though; I have to, every day.

Someone's eyes are on me, I know it. I scan the room. Eventually my eyes light on Kilgour and Elvis: Elvis nods and gets up.

'Murray, you need a change of clothes.'

He looks at the empties,

'You won't be driving, then? Very well, you'll take my car. Sgt Wilson is out front. The code is 'Smokescreen'. Get her to drive you home. Back by 5.'

'Northwood and back? By five. I'll do my very best...sir.'

Elvis clenches his fist. Walks off. I feel even better.

'Lucky you!' gets bellowed in my ear.

Great! Former pride of the Namibian Police force, Frikkie Du Toit -Fritz the Twat to his acquaintances – has been earwigging. The not-quite-Japie drone goes on:

'All afternoon with the ACC's pet kaffir. Going to get yourself some dark chocolate?'

I barge past him. He laughs at my back. I get in the BMW, one of the newest cars the Met has. It is 5 years old.

'Hi, Joyous. Elvis says 'smokescreen'. Drive me home, would you? Apparently, I'm not presentable enough.' I hold out my lapels with finger and thumb.

'Northwood isn't it?' Sgt Joyous Wilson asks.

'Yeah, back by five.'

She snorts. Guns the motor.

I want to talk.

'What the fuck are you doing in the Met, Joy? '

'It's a job, isn't it? More than a lot of people have.'

'How long have you been in?'

'12 years.'

'2003? You must have noticed then?'

'What?'

'How white was your intake at the Police College?'

'60, 70%, why?'

'How many whites at our nick?'

Joyous Wilson shrugs. 'Does it matter?'

'It should.'

We're quiet for a while. I look at the piles of rubbish in the streets. Kids looking through likely piles for something, anything.

'There are laws. Murray. No racist comments, no discrimination...'

'Oh yeah, there are. I bet you've never heard the n-word.'

'Not from Whitey.'

'What do you think the wankers do behind your back? Christ, you wouldn't belie-'

'Does a tree fall in the wood?' The conversation is over.

I come out with three coat-hangers' full draped over my shoulder. The door has slammed behind me. My wife, Yolanda, has said a grand total of two sentences to me, in the half-hour it's taken to shave, shower and get my shit together. I'm almost at the car when the patter of trainers precedes a pair of arms wrapped tight around my thighs. I kneel down and look at my beautiful daughter, Victoria, and wonder again at the chocolate-drp[eyes and at how different they are from my pictish blues.

'Stay, Dad.' She says, and a tear darkens her skin several shades.

I slam the car-boot lid, the clothes are in a heap inside. I sit next to Joyous, who's looking at me like I've grown a second nose:

'There's always someone to hear the tree fall.' I say. 'Drive.'

Joyous dropped me off. I rapped on the window.

'What's this 'Smokescreen' shit?'

'Don't you know?' She laughed and drove off to a parking bay.

My carefully chosen changes of clothes didn't enjoy the journey, but at least they were clean. Apart from the Press having departed, nothing much had changed in the Commons' Bar. The barman still looked bored. The TV was still on, but no-one was watching. Kilgour was sitting alone, looking smug. The ACC wasn't in sight. I headed off to the lav to get changed. Elvis came out wiping the back of his hand across his nose. His eyes glittered:

'Back already? Well done.'

And it was. Joy had driven fast and decisively and knew her A-Z, or at least which bits of it were accurate, nowadays. Not even police cars had satnav.

I got changed. Hung the spare and dirty clothing on the hook in a cubicle. Checked my mobile for power. Just a quarter of battery left. It beeped. Another message: didn't recognise the number.

'12.15. Report 2 me. B4 M-'nite. Station. McCracken.'

I reckoned if I laid off the booze until then I'd be alright to drive. Shame Harry had bailed out.

The three uniforms were carrying office-type furniture in. Cubicle partitioning was being set up to imitate a wall behind a desk. A BBC crew were watching in the background, ready with lights, camera, waiting for the action. Elvis pulled me close, spoke into my ear, his breath moving the hairs:

'Ray Murray: this is your moment, you're going to be on the telly.'

'What for?'

'Can't you guess? I bet you know your lines when I give you the cue.'

Then the ACC and I sat behind a desk, microphones in front of us, for all the world as if a real press conference was taking place. There was even a nameplate on the desk for me.

Elvis kicked off:

'I have been asked to make a statement concerning the investigation into the circumstances of the Prime Minister's sudden demise...'

I wondered where this kind of language came from; did anyone - ever - really speak like this, unless they were reading from a script? The letters on the autocue were massive: death of royalty size; Needles explained some of the old typesetters' nicknames for font sizes once. Elvis obviously needed glasses, but wouldn't wear them for the Telly.

'...new evidence has come to light which completely exonerates the Home Secretary. I now hand you over to my colleague Detective Inspector Ray Murray, CID for a brief explanation...'

I glanced at the autocue. It was completely blank. Elvis' head was down, pretending to look at important papers, a hint of a smirk was still visible. To me at least. I cleared my throat.

'The Home Secretary was helping myself in the course of another enquiry at the time of the Prime Minister's death.'

The cameras stopped rolling. Elvis looked at me like I was a dog who'd mastered a difficult trick. It was easy, in the end. Except I didn't actually know the Time of Death, did I?

The BBC crew left. I turned to Elvis:

'That it then?'

'Yes, that will be all. The Home Secretary mentioned a tape..?'

'Oh that. The recorder didn't work, last one in the building, sir. Shame, eh?'

'A shame it is.'

He gave me a look that said he was quite sure it was a shame for me.

It was getting on for a quarter to 6. I cupped my hands over my nose and mouth, breathed out. Not sweet, not too strong. I headed out to the company car. I could always say the magic word if I was stopped:

'Smokescreen' – maybe I'd find out what it meant if I said it to enough people.

Chapter 6

A Message for Demetrios

The car found its way to Soho; I was hungry. Greek Street was reasonably safe and it wasn't yet dark. I parked up. Went to a cheap looking place, 'Bazalgette's'. It was close enough to Shaftesbury to prefer Euros, but deep enough in Soho not to be choosy, especially if the customer was Old Bill. It was dark inside; there was a couldn't-put-your-finger-on-it smell; it was recognisable, but probably in the wrong place. The waitress wasn't Polish, but her parents were. She was about 18 in the figure and forty in the face.

'One is it?'

'One's enough.'

'Window seat?'

'No thanks, near the bar.'

'Drink?'

'Yes, I do.'

'What - would - Sir - like?'

'Just bring a beer you chippy cow!'

She crumpled and I knew I needed that drink. The resentful waitress brought the beer and left the menu in front of me. The lasagne was cheap and tasted like it, I left an extravagant tip, a pile of sterling notes. No-one wished me goodnight as I left.

Berwick Street was around the corner. I fancied a drink in Harry Xeno's brother's club. Xeno was Harry's smoking handle: in the illicit smoke-easys most people use an assumed name. His real name was Aristotle Chryssipous, making his brother Demetrios Chryssipous – a name known to us, as we used to say in press statements. Demetrios' club was one of several he owned, but the one on Berwick Street was his first. Naturally enough, the lurid blue neon outside said 'The One Club'.

I flashed my warrant card at the door and said:

'Ari sent me, got a message for Demetrios.'

The heavy grunted, pointed at the bar. A barman called 'Boss!' through a curtain behind. Demitrios came out. He looked nothing like his brother: Ari/Harry looked like a comedy Greek, all moustache and gold - teeth and wrist-wear. His brother looked like what he was, a successful businessman.

'Ari's partner, isn't it? Drink?'

'On duty.'

'You do, don't you: Ari says.'

He plonked a bottle of Ouzo and two egg-cup sized glasses in front of us.

'So,' he said, pouring generous measures for both of us. 'To what do I owe...You know how it goes.'

'Nothing much. I was in the area.'

He raised an eyebrow and yammed the ouzo. Had the bottle ready and aimed for the next. I followed suit, coughed a little afterwards. The glasses were filled.

'Try again, Ray.'

'Seen Ari recently?'

'What's recently?'

'Dunno, when the Spaniard came in and argued over the extras?'

The ouzos were summarily emptied and recharged.

'Ray, I mean no offence, but what the fuck are you on about?'

I picked up first this time. Grabbed the bottle when the burn stopped.

'You know Demi, I have no idea...'

'Costas, bring Mr Murray a snack!' The barman went through the curtain.

'Ray, stay, have a nibble, watch the early show, it starts at seven. Do me a favour, though, don't drink any more, hey?'

He fled behind the curtain.

Costas slammed a plate of figs on the table in front of me. I turned to the stage, dead-eyed.

10 o'clock. I had left the club. Helen of Troy had been the first act. Helen of Amstelveen more like. Six feet two of Amazonian Hollander blonde. Still, whoever saw a Greek girl 'dancing' in a Soho club. I got a good 2 hours kip though, and I was grateful to Demetrios for that, at least. Still a bit fuzzy though, I couldn't quite remember where I'd left the car. Had to be somewhere near that restaurant. Greek Street, wasn't it?

It was. The not-Polish waitress was leaning against the wing, smoking.

'Put that out, are you mad? I could arrest you.'

'You can't get the smell out of your clothes you know.'

She blew a cloud at me. I snatched the cigarette and threw it as far as I could. It missed the rubbish mounds and landed in a puddle, hissing with rage.

'Listen, Miss. You'd better be on your way.'

'You could help me on it. I need a lift. The commis left without me. We had a fight.'

'I'm on duty. Things to do, places to go.'

'I'm sure it's on your way.'

She gave me a hard-eyed look, a look more common a few hundred yards away. I unlocked the car. She got in. So did I. I gunned the motor.

'Where to?'

'One of those places to go.'

'Right. Hang on. I'm in a hurry.'

She put her arm through mine as we walked into the Slug and Lettuce. The Wharf was superficially unchanged. Suited and booted types drinking madly, braying loudly. Power-dressed women in groups of their own or with the simulacra of city types. No-one here was actually in finance at all. Every single body, mostly actors or the unemployed, was bought and paid for by the Tourist Board. The drinks were, mostly, soft - and the suits on both sexes were stained and threadbare in places. I hoped Needles would be on time. My emergency Euro-stash was nothing like as thick as Harry Xeno's roll had been.

We sat at a table. A waiter came, pencil poised;

'Gin and tonic. Bombay Sapph.' She smiled at me.

'I'll have the same... and an espresso, double shot.'

'Aren't you going to ask my name?' she said.

'I don't care what it is.'

She put her hand on my thigh:

'Neither do I.'

Needles stumbled in, right on time, looking a little conspicuous. It wasn't just the misbuttoned denim. More the swelling round the eyes and nose and the bloodstains on that jacket. I waved him over. Whistled a waiter; very Flaming Lamborghini; ordered Needles a double malt. He sat opposite keeping the disc of the table top between him and my companion.

'Confidential, you said.' He darted a look at the Non-Pole.

'Bye, lover-boy thanks for the ride.' She bee-lined for the more exotic Japanese at the far end of the
room.

'It just wasn't meant to be.' I said.

Needles necked his nip, rattled the glass on the table top. I waved at a waiter.

'What happened to you?'

'After the Commons Bar, I was driving to the office. Got pulled over. Bill. Uniforms. Got a kicking and a gnomic warning.'

'Eh??'

'They said: "Passive smoking's dangerous, careful about the company you keep."'

'Sounds pretty gnomic, whatever that is. That's it though, no explanation?'

'I heard something, when I was lying doggo, on the pavement.'

'What?'

'I'm not sure, I had my hands over my head, it was indistinct.'

'Spit it out, you fucker!'

'"Smokescreen," I think it was. Yeah, Smokescreen.'

I sat silent. Needles was itchy, twitchy, the questions ready to burst out of him. I held up a hand.

'Let me think, hey?'

The cool, bluey gin tasted good. I could have done another 3 there and then.

'Let me tell you a story, the kind that stays out of newspapers...'

Needles got a small digital recorder out of the denim Jacket pocket. I shook my head and outlined the events leading up to the visit of the HomeSec to our nick. From the mysterious tip-off to whacking him one.

'You're a fucking Nutter, Murray. A real 'heid the baw', as they say, aren't you?'

'Sometimes I wonder myself.'

'But... no offence, Murray, so what?'

'Didn't you wonder what I was doing with the Task Force? Seen the news on Telly this evening?'

'No, and no,' he pointed at his face, gargoyled by the Uniforms' boots.

'I was busy, remember?'

I explained how I was the HomeSec's alibi, except no-one had said anything about the PM's TOD. Needles' tongue probed a loose tooth, he winced:

'Who do you reckon tipped Harry off, about the cigs I mean?'

'That's what I'd like to know, mate.'

I looked at my watch, 11.30.

'Gotta look sharp, Needles... Got to see my Super at the nick. Keep shtumm. I'll let you know when.'

'Look sharp, ha ha. Who's your Super? Oh yeah... McCrackers. Well good luck.'

I threw my last Euros on the table for the bill. The Non-Pole winked as I left, her arms linked with the Japanese businessmen on either side: a little foreign exchange transaction in prospect.

Chapter 7

"I knew he wanted you there, Elvis."

The car and plenty of rubber abandoned in front of the Station, I bounded up the steps, almost bowled McCrackers over on the other side of the door. He wasn't in uniform. Wax Jacket and brogues: he
looked dressed to shout abuse at the England Rugby XV at Twickers. Funny how sport still went on; persuading people that life was normal. What was it? Opium for the people. A religious experience in
more ways than one.

'Careful, Murray, what's your hurry?' He laughed, I wasn't sure why.

'It's five to, Sir. I only just made it.'

'Just one more, was it?'

'Something like that.'

His eyes were the worst. Some rugby incident had detached a retina; he was blind in one eye. This one always seemed to follow you, no matter where he was actually looking. He really did look like some hellfire Protestant preacher. The Belfast accent made it worse; good Fenian McCrackers would have been mortified to know it.

'My office.'

And I puffed following him up the stairs, he'd stayed fit, even though the last scrummage was long ago.

We sat in his dull, monochrome office. I'd been thinking on the drive over. How much should I tell him? The only cannon in the nick looser than I was.

'Well?'

'You saw the news?'

'I did.'

He reached into the drawer. Pulled out a bottle, and two dainty stemmed glasses. It was fucking sherry. I'd have laughed if I'd dared. He poured.

'I knew he wanted you there, Elvis.'

His accent made it come out "Eyal-vuss", and he bit it off and spat it out, expelling around 30 years of rivalry and bitterness. He went on:

'I just wanted to know why. Only one way to find out.'

'Send me?'

'Just so. And so?'

He gave a little smile, as though he found the word play amusing.

'Well, Sir, it's just about how it looks.'

'Just about?'

'Well, there's a couple of things... No-one else but me and and DS Chryssipous knew anything about the contraband cigs. Not even the Revenue.'

'Customs didn't know, hmm? So you're wondering where the tip-off came from?'

And I thought to myself: you crafty old bugger; wondered how much of the anger was a management tool, and how valuable he found it. I sipped the old lady's drink.

'Yes, sir. And it's the lack of real police work, interviews, forensic, path report. I mean, they might have done it... but Task Force HQ is... well it's
like a Christmas tree display in a shop window: there are the presents all wrapped, lying around it, but the boxes are all empty.'

'Who's the senior officer, apart from Elvis?'

'Me, I suppose...' I felt something horrific was somewhere just out of sight.

'Get the files. Point out you're 2 IC, poke the nest, see what the ants bring out.'

'Yessir.'

'Don't let me down.' It was a dismissal.

Down at the front desk, I used the phone to call Harry's home phone. Unavailable. The lines were probably down or water had got into an exchange. I texted his mobile.

'00.25. Meet. Urgent. Number Six, Noon.'

I launched it into the void with a thumb. He'd get it, or he wouldn't, he'd be there, or he wouldn't. I'd need about a packet of twenty after a morning with Elvis, anyway.

I climbed in the motor and left for the Commons Bar, heading for the spare clothes and maybe some kip on those velvet banquettes. One of the uniforms would be manning the phones until lights out, maybe he'd lend me his toothbrush.

Chapter 8

The Thompson Twins

At 8.30 I woke up, when I hit the floor. It wasn't far to fall, but it was a shock. Especially as I looked up to a smirking Fritz the Twat standing over me, arms full of files.

'Rise and shine, Murray. Work to do.'

'Guv to you. Your arsehole hasn't healed up yet has it?'

His eyes narrowed:

'No.'

'Well, I still outrank you then, DS Du Toit. So fuck off out of my face.'

He strode off. 3 uniforms and a DC were humping metal desks and filing cabinets about. Evidently I'd slept through the removal of the bar's portable furniture. The partitioning that had formed the backdrop to yesterday's press statement had lists, photographs and a pin-marked map fastened to it. The ACC had a mobile welded to his ear, giving someone a good listening to. Why did people nod, when they were on the 'phone?

I hauled myself off the floor. The duty plod had been awake when I'd arrived last night. He took a few Guinness with me, in the end. No sign of him this morning. I'd asked him about 'Smokescreen.' Couldn't remember his answer. Not right then. I needed coffee. The urn was in, on a table with tubular legs over by the bar. A jar of the chicory-heavy instant coffee that was all you could get now had the lid off and a spoon periscope-d out of it. The paper cups were still in a shrink-wrapped sleeve. No hot water yet then.

A quarter pint of the uniform's last Guinness sat on the bar. I picked it up. Headed for the lav. Put the glass on the sink unit. I knelt before the porcelain and waited for the flood. When the convulsions were over, I kept my eyes shut as I flushed the evidence away. The Guinness mouthwash almost set me off again, but not quite.

In the bar, something approaching an operations centre had finally taken shape. The eight-man team were in a semi-circle around Elvis, who swept an arm in my direction:

'Gentlemen, your Task Force leader: DI Ray Murray.'

There was a ripple of grunts, 'guvs' and one 'old red-eyes is back'. The PCs were first to introduce themselves;

'PC Grant, guv. Just left traffic.' No nights, for her.

'PC Abramowicz. ... I'm on probation, Sir.' Great.

'PC Hewson, guv.' Fuck me George Hewson, DS on the Drugs Squad, last I'd heard. I nodded at him.

There were two DC's whose names I couldn't be bothered to remember. Close cropped hair and ungenerous mouths. I mentally tagged them the Thompson Twins. The other DC I knew of: Johnny

Wright, 'Johnny-on-the-spot', he'd worked with Harry in the past. My partner had never explained the nickname. That left the two DS's

'DS Wilton, guv.' I looked down at him. He was 5ft 2 inches in his lifts. Of course, his nickname was 'Off-Cut.'

'DS Du Toit, guv. Welcome aboard.'

'Man the fucking lifeboats.' I said to no-one in particular.

'Murray, a word.' Elvis was tugging at my Jacket. I shrugged him off: almost overbalanced. We stepped off to one side.

'You report to me. All the files are here, everything. All in order. I want this wrapped up by the weekend. You understand?'

'Understand what, sir? The hurry?'

'Someone as unsteady on their feet as you should avoid skating on thin ice.'

He headed out of the building, striding long, like someone who never had to look down for pitfalls - or thin ice.

One of the three metal desks had my nameplate from the TV broadcast on it. And the pile of files Fritz the Twat had been carrying. I shouted:

'Oy! Who's going to brief me on the investigation then?'

Off-Cut started to step forward, but Du Toit put an arm out and Wilton's chest rebounded off it.

'I'll do it, Guv. Senior member of the team and all that.'

We sat on opposite sides of the desk and the pile of files. All police work makes paper: that's why there are so few charges or even arrests. Important investigations just make more of it. I had no intention of reading every sheet.

'Abramowicz! Two coffees, please, black' It came out as a croak.

'I'll have white.' No please from Fritz the Twat, naturally.

'Give. What have you got?'

'PM found on the ground outside, out front of here. No blood. No obvious wound.'

'CCTV?' I asked.

Fritz laughed; 'Yeah, right up until lights out. Nothing conclusive.'

'But something?'

'If you call an outline shape something; bending over the body. There must have been an outage earlier too, there's a 20 minute blank. No body: body there. Alakazam!'

'Any corroboration on the power cut?'

'Barman says yes.'

'What about the extent, all of the Palace of Westminster, just this building? What?'

'It'll be in the file.' He didn't know.

'You been on this from the beginning?'

'No...' he looked over my shoulder, at Churchill or Palmerston for all I knew.

'Just since yesterday morning.'

'Anybody from the initial discovery?'

'No.'

'Send the Thompson Twins to find out about the power.'

'Eh?'

'Those two, the DCs.'

I pointed at them. They still looked joined at the hip. Fritz went over to give them their orders. My coffee arrived. Good. Looked like I had to do some reading after all.

Things appeared on my desk from time to time. A telephone, one of the laptops from the hastily knocked-up network, more coffee. Most of the files ended up on the floor. By 11.15, I had 3 documents in front of me: An initialled statement by one AB of Westminster Security, the privatised force that protected the Palace from terrorists. Mostly ex-Bill, Army and in a few cases Special Forces: they had adopted a policy of anonymity, after an Internet beheading in 2013. The Guardian, before it folded, had dubbed them the Praetorian Guard.

There was a SOCO's report, unsigned, with a note clipped to the front 'Body moved?' Lastly, the autopsy report. The doctor said TOD was uncertain, within 5 hours of the body's discovery. I didn't understand the science.

I spotted Abramawicz, over by the door, examining something from his ear;

'Oy! Abramawicz, got something for you to do.'

To his credit, he looked pleased. I handed him the documents.

'See if you can't find a photocopier somewhere. 2 copies of all of it. Give it to me personally.'

I pictured him wandering about aimlessly for a quarter of an hour before plucking up the courage to ask someone who might be able to help him.

Fritz appeared in front of the desk.

'What time we knocking off tonight, Guv?'

'How do I know?'

'I'm meeting some guys... we're over Southall, tonight. Going for an Indian.'

'Do what you like.'

They wouldn't be debating the merits of Korma over Vindaloo: sometimes I just got too tired to care. Even about the mayhem Fritz and his thug pals would cause in the South Asian Enclave.

Amazingly, Abramawicz turned up with the documents: the copies in a new file. I thanked him. He needed to find another line of work. Such efficiency wouldn't go unpunished long. I headed to the lavs to pick up my spare clothes. It was time to go and meet Harry at the Number Six. I fumbled the coathangers, my best Jacket fell in a puddle of piss by the pedestal. As I picked it up a bulging creamy envelope fell out.

I recognised the embossed crest from quite a few previous communications. A post-it note's glue had dried and the note itself fell out as I unfolded the letter:

'From the Office of the Nigerian State Required Skills Immigration Scheme...

Dear Mr Murray,

We are pleased at your interest in the NSRSIS. However, we regret to inform you that your particular field's quota is full. We encourage you to reapply, but can at present give you no indication as to when your application might be accepted.

In the meantime, there are two other possibilities open to you.

Please find enclosed appropriate paper work for a) and b)'

Etc, Etc. I thought. I looked at the post-it note

'Ray,

Unless it stops, it's option b)

Yol.'

I stuffed all the paper in the pocket of the damp jacket, headed outto the car.

Chapter 9

"Like the song, eh?"

The paper burned quite well, an inch square at a time. Woodbine didn't look pleased at this use of one of his ashtrays. Harry walked in. A face like a man with toothache.

'She's going, Harry.' I said.

'Who? Yol?'

'Who else?'

'Camberwell?'

'Nigeria.'

He nodded : '"Roots Initiative" is it?'

'Didn't have you down as a Daily Mail reader, Harry.'

'Everybody calls it that now.'

'Roots is a book about an African-American returning to the Gambia. Different countries, dummy.'

'Like the song, eh?'

He started humming an old 70's song, you'd hear it on Capital Super Gold 70's any day of the week. Odyssey sang it. A heavy ashtray crashed onto the bar in front of Harry.

'That's enough.' Woodbine said.

'You never fancy it? Woodbine?'

Harry was wielding a big shovel, the hole wasn't big enough yet.

'He's trying my patience, Ray.' Woodbined growled.

'Carlton's family's from Kingston, you fuckwit.'

Harry's toothache looked worse.

Woodbine disappeared into the back room.

'Nigeria, I don't understand it.' Harry said.

'What, here's better?' I raised my eyebrows.

'Yeah, they've got the oil, it's a rich country, but...'

'But what Harry? They have multi-party elections and the voters get to the booths on their own'

'Still...' He wasn't convinced, and never would be.

'What're you going to do?'

'Maybe I'll enter the White Card Lottery, get in that way.'

'Yol won't help... What about Vic?'

'The lottery was Yol's suggestion.'

Harry changed the subject.

'What did you want? I'm on the sick.'

'The tip-off, about the fags? Anonymous was it?'

He considered this. 'Could say that.'

'Phone call, smokesignal, what?'

'Thing is, there was a piece of paper on my desk, in CID.'

'And where is this evidence, Harry?'

'In the bin. Where else?'

'Great... so we've no idea where it's from?'

I scattered the remaining paper like confetti over Harry.

'I know exactly where it came from. It was on headed paper.' Harry said.

'I get it. Didn't sign it as well, did he?'

Harry shrugged.

'Take the car back to the nick, Harry, and fuck off!'

I called to him as he reached the door.

'Aristotle!'

He turned, surprised at hearing his Sunday name.

'It's true what they say isn't it?'

'What?'

'Beware of Greeks bearing gifts.' I turned back to the bar, motioned for a drink.

Chapter 10

Task Force

The light hurt. Even in the slub-grey rain. It was after two. The street was deserted outside the Number Six. A car pulled up. An unmistakable brogue rang out:

'Get in Murray, ye sot!' McCrackers. Great. I did as I was told.

'Homeless now is it? Takin' yer clothes with ye?'

I shoved my coat-hangered clothes in the back seat. Breathed out heavily, hoping to upset the secret sherry drinker. No such luck.

'I'd like a report, daily, Murray.'

'I was going to ring later.'

'From the "Task Force HQ"? Right! Why don't I invite Elvis to meet us face to face?'

The coarse floridity in his face hardened to brick. Then his features relaxed, the moment for control past.

'How many of you are there? Eight.?'

'Plus me.'

'Task Force!' He snorted. Shook his head.

I stared out of the window. Peeling posters for concerts, sports events and even political rallies gave the rain-dulled walls a diseased look. London, the grand metropolis; if only it still were. McCrackers was talking at me:

'I retire in three months.'

'Congratulations.'

He took his good eye off the road momentarily. Weighed my response.

'Yeah, well. Won't be fockin' Marbella will it? Won't even be fockin' Margate!'

I looked at him out of the corner of my eye:

'Mourne?'

'Not even there.' But he smiled.

'35 years. 1980. Imagine: Belfast Bhoy joins the Met.'

'Why not the RUC?'

'We'll have a chat in my office.'

'Is that wise?'

'Oh no, you'll report to me when we get back in the car. There's something you need in the station.'

And he went somewhere a long way away for the rest of the trip. Maybe Marbella, maybe somewhere equally unreachable, from far-away-almost-55

We were in that low-status office again. I hadn't liked the quiet in the car: almost preferred the noisy unpredictability. He laid both palms flat on the desk:

'Got a personal weapon?'

'In the armoury.'

'Don't be daft! You know what I mean.'

'I share – shared a pump action with Harry. We kept it in the car.'

'You need one.'

He opened a drawer. What looked like 10 pounds of extremely old fashioned metalwork crashed onto the desk in front of me.

'What's that? An antique?'

'It's a Webley Mark VI. My father's.'

'Army?'

'RUC.'

I digested that for a second or two. Felt brave:

'So?'

The palms were flat on the desk again: now they looked like they were trying to push the desk into the floor.

'He did 35 years too. Retired as Inspector, not bad for a Catholic. Could have written that on his tombstone. When I said I wanted to join, he said "Don't do it, Douglas.' I asked him why: he said no-one should find human faeces in their locker at the end of a night shift, not even in Belfast.'

He took several deep breaths. I stayed quiet.

'Thing is, a week after retirement, he shot himself with that gun.'

My hand, which had - I admit- been toying with it as it lay on the desktop, jerked away.

'Keep it.' He said. He stood: 'Let's get back to the car, you can tell me what's up.'

Jerry Patel was on the desk. The station was crowded, not with arrested criminals, of course. Just officers keeping out of the rain. I felt a little guilty about the broken promise to talk to Elvis. I leaned close over the reception desk, kept my voice low.

'Jerry, got any rellies in the Enclave?'

'Yeah, my in-laws are in Southall.'

'Give 'em a ring. Stay in tonight. There might be trouble.'

Jerry just nodded: it had been risky to say so much in front of so many of our colleagues. I gave him a thumbs up and followed McCrackers out of the building.

We were parked in front of 'Babylon-On-Thames' on the other side of Vauxhall Bridge. Maybe McCrackers was being funny, wanting his report in front of MI6's building. Or maybe it meant nothing, and I was paranoid, since I hadn't had a drink for quite a few hours. I gave him the file, offered to let him keep one of the two copies of the docs. He shook his head.

'What do you think?' he asked me.

'Something's iffy. It definitely isn't a proper investigation. It's a cover-up or something.'

He looked at me, smiled. A scary smile, OK, but a smile.

'A smokescreen, perhaps?'

There was nothing to say to that. I got out of the car, the spare clothes rolled in a ragged bundle now, precariously held together with a belt. The passenger window slid down, McCrackers leaned towards it:

'If you get the chance, ask Elvis about his old nickname, from our first nick, after Hendon. In '82.'

And the car splashed my trousers as he drove away.

Big Ben, or a 4-year old recording of it, struck four. The loudspeakers were small and discreet, the tourists barely knew the difference. By the time I got to the Commons' Bar, Fritz was looking anxious to leave. The Thompson Twins were gone. Off-Cut was over-compensating with Grant; chatting-up the PC who was studying the jerry-built Murder Wall over his shoulder. I doubted whether anything fascinating had been posted on it since I left.

McCrackers hadn't helped much, apart from the gun. A smoke-screen, for what? What did they have to hide? And who was hiding it with an investigation, as half-hearted as it was, into the death of a Prime Minister? I didn't know. Grant caught my eye, barged past Off-Cut. He looked used to it.

'Sir, took a call from your wife: she says don't bother calling. It's not urgent any more. And she said –'

At this point she looked up into space, like a schoolgirl about to recite:

'"Do you feel lucky, drunk?" She said you know what it meant.'

'Yeah, I know what it means. Stop 'Sir'-ring me up. Guv'll do.'

She nodded nervously. Seemed about to take this as dismissal. I said:

'Got a nickname, then?'

'Yeah. They call me Loan. The knackered old shits used to call me Student Grant. One day I said what the fuck's that? They just laughed and started calling me "Student Loan". Just Loan now.'

'Got a degree then, have you?'

'Yes Guv, I was fast-track until they cancelled the programme.'

I wondered if she'd still be paying her loan off on retirement.

'You going now too?'

'Uhm, nooo...'

'Knocking off at Midnight? Plenty of time to get home before lights out, is it?'

'Not my idea, Guv. Federation rules. Not insured, if anything happens, are we.'

She lifted her chin. She was right, I was being an arsehole.

'Got a change of clothes with you?'

I knew she had. Policewomen did not travel in uniform; Federation rules. She nodded.

'Get ready then. You're my driver from now on.'

'What about lights out, the Fed?'

'"Smokescreen."' I said. She looked blank. Good. I went on.

'Anybody - police, Praetorian, the British Transport Police - asks: just say "Smokescreen."'

'What's it mean, Guv?'

'AbraCadabra, Open Sesame, Alakazam: take your pick.'

She went off to the bogs to change. Outside the building she asked:

'Which car?'

'Yours.'

She rolled her eyes and took me over to a 10 year old convertible Mini.

'Discreet.' I said.

'Graduation present.'

'What, from new?'

'6 months old, when I got it.'

'Nice present.'

'My uncle. He does okay. It's still a present: he pays to keep it going.'

He must have been doing okay; my soon-to-be ex-wife and I had a car, yes: but it was a 15 year old wreck and just managed to ferry Yolanda from the house to the surgery and back. Pretty poor for a DI and a GP. We'd had a new BMW once. It seemed a long time ago.

'Where to?'

'Millbank. Round the back. I'll show you.'

The Mini was in good nick. The engine sounded sweet and the gear-changes sounded crisp but smooth. 'Loan' pulled up outside a portakabin inside a razor wired compound. A sign hung loosely from the wire gate :'Westminster Security'. I got out. Turned and motioned Grant to follow. I rang the bell.

It was answered by one of the Thompson Twins' cousins. Ex-Army or SF I guessed: not Bill. He just looked expectantly, safe on the other side of the locked gate.

'DI Murray and DC Grant; We want to speak to ex-DCI Andy Bell.'

'Appointment?'

'No, but..'

'No appointment, no chance. Fuck off.'

'Loan' didn't look too surprised by her promotion. She raised an eyebrow at me and enunciated carefully at the muscle:

'Smokescreen.'

The muscle grunted and let us in. 'Loan' said out of the side of her mouth as we crunched over the gravel:

'Now that's magic!'

We were shown into an office with furniture as cheap and temporary-looking as the building. Both had been on site for several years. 'Temporarily permanent' like so many things in the last ten years or so. Andy Bell's hair had been styled in the company cut, cropped short. He looked leaner than when he'd been my Guv,

but that change had coincided with his stint in the Met VIP Security Squad. I supposed he was a natural choice for the 'Praetorians'. He wasn't the top-man, or even the deputy, but most of CID had heard rumours he would be one day. I'd liked him, he'd been a good boss, better than most. No nickname, just initials.

'What is it, Ray?'

'This is DC Grant.' AB raised an eyebrow.

'I'm quite busy, nowadays.' He said.

I glanced at the gorilla from the gate, who hadn't quite got around to leaving. AB made a brushing motion at him with the fingers of one hand.

'So?' He leaned forward. That had been it, I remembered. The secret of his management skills; the way you felt you had every atomically-sized bit of his attention, for however short a period.

'Well, AB. You sent me a message.'

'What?'

'On the report, the PM's corpse. You guys sign them off with your service number, don't you? Bit of a risk with the anonymity, eh? Who else would the initials AB mean?'

'Oh God! You're heading the Enquiry?'

'Thanks. Don't you watch the TV?'

'I'd heard it was a DI Murray, but - no offence Ray- I never for one moment thought it was you!'

'Why?' I asked, but I knew, really.

'Had a drink today, Ray?' He moved a hand, presumably towards a desk-drawer.

'No... umm...' I dry swallowed. 'I'm cutting down.'

'Sure, you are.' He said.

He thought better of the drawer, or maybe it had been a tease.

'Fuck it. In for a penny, eh? You know the corpse was moved?'

'It looks that way.'

'It is that way.' The hand went back to the drawer.

'Not for me.' It came out shaky.

An ancient SmartDisk dropped on the desk in front of me. 32MB. Wouldn't have much on it, I supposed.

'And?'

'We run the CCTV.'

'Is it the missing footage?'

'It's some missing footage.'

'Of what?'

'That's your lot, Ray. Can you lose that report? Get shot of my initials. If a drunk can work it out, anyone can, hmm?'

'You know Elvis is involved?'

He just smiled and nodded. Then jerked his head towards the door.

Chapter 11

The Honorable Member

Back at the Commons Bar, the Thomson Twins were back. They and Off-Cut were hanging on to every word coming out of a short, portly guy about 60 years old. And there were a lot of them; words that is. His face was puce from a lifetime of drink or maybe he was just short of breath.

'Who the fuck are you?' I said.

'Gilbert Hardacre, the Honorable Member for...'

'For I don't care where. This is a police investigation and the Bar is closed.'

'I am a Member of Parliament and it is my inalienable right to ...'

'I remember those. Think I used to have some. You remember them, guys?'

The Thompson Twins both clenched their fists. God! Were they really twins? Off-Cut seemed to be trying to make himself even smaller. Grant was smirking. I picked the Honorable Member up by the collar and the seat of his pants; he was not as heavy as he looked. He wriggled a bit. We were half-way to the door, when Elvis came in:

'What's going on?' he said.

The hon. Member started to bluster. I gave him a shake.

'This gentleman is just leaving. I've explained the bar is closed.'

Elvis cleared his throat. Ran a finger round his collar:

'I'm afraid the Detective Inspector is correct. I'm sorry, Sir.'

'Thought so. Just doesn't have the password, eh?'

I kept hold of the MP until we were outside, where I let him go; like all windbags should he meandered away on the breeze, still talking.

I went back to the erstwhile audience:

'You can go. See you at 8 tomorrow.'

The close cropped heads nodded uneasily; seemed to look over at Elvis, who was behind my desk, looking in drawers. Off-Cut was gone on the 'to-' of 'tomorrow.' I whispered to Grant:

'Thin out, go to the bog or something. Safer.'

She did, after I gave her a shove.

'Anything I can help you with Sir?'

'I doubt that very much.' Elvis said. But he stopped rifling my desk.

'Sir, why am I in charge of this investigation? Why do we have a grand total of 8 officers assigned to an investigation into a Prime Minister's death?'

'There are more urgent matters. It's a question of priorities. I'm sure you'll achieve a satisfactory result.'

'Priorities? Is that some kind of joke, sir?'

'Keep your eye on the news, Inspector. That's all I can say.'

He got up. Walked his confident walk all the way out of the building.

Grant came out of the Ladies'. I wondered if she'd heard anything. I thought my desk was far enough away. I hunted behind the bar for the barman's telly. We still had his keys for the bar. I laughed at the thought of it.

'What's so funny, Guv?' Grant had her head to one side.

'Kid – sweetshop?'

I rattled the barman's keys in her face. She made a grab. I made sure she missed.

'I ... can... handle... it.'

She flinched. Went off and made a show of tidying my desk. I turned the TV on. Dropping the Smart Disk on my desk in front of her, I said:

'Please, see if any of the laptops can do anything with this.'

And I went to the bar to check out the state of the nation. Somehow, I'd got to 8 pm without a drink. I'd have to have one soon or it could get messy. The continuity voice said:

'We interrupt this programme to go live to the Cabinet Office, where the Pro-Tem Prime Minister Foreign Secretary Carlton is about to give a statement..'

No 'Jackie'. It had to be serious then. The woman appeared, she looked ragged, the make-up people hadn't fixed her hair right, or she hadn't let them.

'Earlier this evening there was a series of incidents in the South Asian Enclave. There were reports of armed gangs smashing windows. Several Mosques and temples have been razed. There are clashes on-going as I speak. The Rapid Reaction Force has been mobilised by the Chiefs-Of-Staff and should be in a position to facilitate a containment of the situation by midnight. In order to preserve and protect the general public the curfew is now to cover the hours of darkness with immediate effect. In the interest of National Security, all curfew breakers will be detained. I remind you that persons arrested in connection with National Security may be detained for up to 56 days in accordance with PACE Code H section 24a, amendment i).

We ask that you all remain calm at this difficult time.'

I switched it off. Jesus! Was that what Fritz and his pals had been up to? Reenacting *Krystallnacht* in the South Asian Enclave. Why?

'Miles away, eh? Better come and look at this Guv.'

I followed Grant to one of the other desks. Fritz's, as it happened. The laptop looked a bit newer than the others.

'A card reader. Doubt Fritz even knows what it does.'

She laughed bitterly:

'Anyway, take a look.'

She pressed a button, turned the laptop slightly towards me.

The PM was alive, the toothy grin evident as always. He was lying down. On the cabinet office table: naked. 'Jackie' Carlton was leaning over him, showing good ball skills. The footage looked like the soundtrack would have been interesting. 'Jackie' pulled away. Pushed a leather-upholstered carver away from the table. Leaned over it, legs apart. The PM was keen, excited. Too excited. He slipped and fell getting off the table. You could almost hear his head hitting the corner of the heavy table. He looked dead immediately. The thing I'd always remember was the look on 'Jackie' Carlton's face: I'd seen it too many times myself. In the bathroom mirror in flats I couldn't remember arriving at.

'Fuck!' I said.

'Was that what it was? I wasn't sure.'

We both laughed. Laughter in the dark.

'Can you trash the laptop? I don't want any trace of that card's contents on there.'

'Look, I'll stick it in the boot of the Mini. We'll chuck it in the Thames tomorrow morning. Another unexplained theft. The Police are busy, aren't they?'

It would have to do.

We took it out to the car. No-one stopped us, but then we were inside the wire at the Palace of Westminster: maybe we hadn't broken the curfew.

In the bar I put the TV back on. There was some footage of street fighting. Could have been that night, could have been archive. It *was* Southall. You could hear sirens in the background, never actually saw a vehicle attached to one. The voice over was droning on about simmering tensions: irresponsible minorities. All the usual clichés. I wondered if it really was all kicking off; if it really was the final countdown for democracy.

'Not murder at least.' Grant offered.

'Probably worse though.'

'What're you going to do?'

'You mean 'have'. What am I going to have?'

'What are you going to have?' She played along.

'A hangover, tomorrow.'

And I turned towards the bar, deciding between Guinness and a good malt and opting for both.

Chapter 12

Tizer and Smokey Bacon

I didn't see that face in the mirror over the Gents' sink the next morning. I'd fantasized about a re-enactment of the CCTV's events with Grant; in the spirit of reconstructing the crime. Held my tongue though, and sat wakeful on the velvet through 'lights out', wondering what the fuck to do. Grant lent me her toothbrush, so I forewent the Guinness mouthwash. She looked like she'd slept on a feather bed. I looked like I'd slept under it. Former DS Doug Hewson was the first uniform in. Raised his eyebrows at seeing us there. I called him over.

'Doug, what...?'
 'Happened? Unlucky, that's all?'
 'What d'you mean?'
 'Caught.'
 'Naaah. Who by?'
 'Fritz. Bang to rights. 60 wraps of coke in the boot.'

'So? It was evidence, right?'

'Against me, yeah.'

'You were dealing?'

'So it would seem.'

'So they busted you and sent you back to uniform?'

'Hey, recruitment's bad.'

'That's bollocks, Doug. When did you start dealing?'

'Didn't I tell you? About when I teamed up with Fritz.'

Doug drifted over to the 'Murder' Wall, stared sightlessly at the pitiful postings.

Since about 2010, uniform and CID had followed US procedure. Officers worked in pairs. For protection, for safety: to keep each other on the straight and narrow. You didn't choose your partner and divorce wasn't an option, not without grounds. Fritz had found his grounds.

The team drifted in. I was surprised everyone had assembled by 10; given the Army on the streets and all. The Thompson Twins probably hadn't had far to come anyway. Fritz was last. He looked a little battered, despite having a big smile on his Afrikaner face. I pointed to his face:

'Argument over the bill? Put too many chapattis on it, did they?'

'You might say that. It was enjoyable even so.'

'Yeah, well. You're staying here tonight. You're manning the room. Got 24 hour kit?'

'I don't think so. It's Chinese tonight.

'You'll do as you're told, DuToit.'

'Smokescreen.'

'Fuck off with that bollocks. Do as you're told, I said'

The smile never wavered.

'We'll see.'

Standing in front of the 'Murder Wall', I asked for any updates. Of course, there was only the Thompson Twins investigation of the power outage, around the time of the discovery of the PM's body.

'Yes, guv: a localised outage...' the one on the left said.

'Only the immediate vicinity affected. The duty building manager...' came from the right.

'says a circuit-breaker was loose. He fixed it himself.' Lefty added.

Christ, they even finished each off each other's sentences. I wondered if they were some experiment released from Porton Down, the government biological warfare research place.

'Call SOCO, Off-Cut, I want a team at the Cabinet Office, ASAP.'

'Roger, Guv.'

'Tell them to give you an ETA, I want to be there.'

The rest of the team looked puzzled. I decided to make some phone calls.

I got hold of Needles at the Standard first:

'Needles, Murray. Might have something for you.'

'I'm chocca. Southall, ring any bells?'

'Even so, I'd like a chat. Somewhere cheaper.'

'Ha! The Hat and Beggar do you?'

'You fucking love those theme pubs don't you?'

'I feel safer among the tourists.'

'Can't be late, dunno how long this curfew's gonna go on, do we?'

'Lunchtime. Journo's lunchtime.'

I hung up, confident of 3 hours in the pub. It was a laugh really, Needles wanted to meet in a mock up of an East End pub: it was down by the Eye. But the Faces there were also unemployed or actors, or both. They staged fights and talked about blags and their muvvers, while the tourists lapped it up.

I tried McCrackers' office; a plummy voice answered:

'Superintendent McCracken's office.'

I hung up.

The hardest call came last. I phoned home. I got the steady buzz of a disconnected line.

I was just considering a pint went Grant approached.

'Better go and deep six that thing, Guv.'

'You a smoker?'

'Naaah. Don't mind the smell, it's the taste.'

'Shame, that. You could always sit outside with some pop and a bag of crisps.'

I collared Off-Cut and told him to text me with a time for SOCO. It would be several hours at least. Grant and I headed out to her car. She followed my directions and we hit the Number Six by 11.15.

'Tizer and smokey bacon, is it?' I said, my hand on the door lever.

'Fuck off, Guv.'

And we got out of her mini and headed into the gloom of Woodbine's bar.

Carlton lit me when we reached the counter. He nodded at Grant:

'Better looking than the Greek. Hope she's got better manners too.'

'She might have, we'll have to see. Guinness for me.'

'Tonic water.'

She looked at me. I felt all the veins in my nose and cheeks and the deep wrinkles and the stubble from no shave. Felt myself failing an inspection. Finally she said:

'Which is worse? The fags or the booze?'

'For my health you mean?'

'No, which addiction. If it was one or the other, I mean. Which would you choose?'

'I think I'd die without either.'

'I know you hadn't had a cig since yesterday.'

'Only yesterday? The law does work you know. I'd smoke a fucking sight more if it was legal.'

'Would you? Would you really? I think you'd just find another law to break, DI Murray.'

'Yeah, well one more fag, then we're off to meet my pet journo.'

'Packet of prawn cocktail, Mr Woodbine. I'll wait outside, Guv.'

Woodbine gave her the crisps and raised his eyebrows at me as she turned away.

Chapter 13

The Hat And Beggar

Grant pulled up at Waterloo Pier. Went round to the boot, pulled out the laptop. Knocked on the passenger side window, pointed towards the water. I watched her pirouette like a discus thrower and then the laptop sailed into the Thames. It was an Olympic standard throw and the white plume as it splashed down was beautiful. She did the silent-movie fake hand-washing thing on the way back. I laughed. It felt good.

Walking to a vacant seat in the Hat and Beggar, Grant's eyes were darting here, there and everywhere: the décor was spot on. Hideously sticky carpet, tobacco
darkened wood. A good trick in a smoke-free zone. We sat in the seating against the wall that me reminded so much of church pews. Admittedly the last time I'd been in a church it had been to buy discount carpets, but even so.

'What do you want this time? Shirley Temple?'

'I'll go, my shout. You'll have a half – of the weakest lager they've got.'

'Fair enough. My round next anyway.'

Grant came back, gingerly slid the glass towards me.

'Don't drink, do you?' I said.

'Not any more.'

She glanced round the pub again:

'Authentic, hey?'

Some beer came down my nose :

'Authentic?? Fuck off, Grant.'

'Look at the skinny ties, the shiny suits.'

I shook my head:

'It looks like a film about the Krays. Even the name of the place... the Hat and Beggar. Shit!'

'What's wrong with that?'

'Jack 'The Hat' McVitie? The Blind Beggar?'

'Sorry Guv, you've lost me.'

'The Blind Beggar was a real pub. In Whitechapel: Ronnie Kray shot one of the Richardson's gang there. McVitie was a minor face in the Krays gang. They went down for him in the end.'

'So what? They're just names.'

'No, they were faces.'

She looked blank.

'Right. Listen. What's the music?'

'I don't fucking know. Guitars, singing. London references.'

'Yeah, the Kinks. My dad liked them.'

'And?' She meant so-fucking-what.

'My dad was a teenager in 1967. The Kray Twins were 34. They liked Dusty, knew Helen Shapiro. They'd have played Julie London on the juke at a push. You'd more likely hear Mantovani than the Kinks.'

'Just details.' She waved a hand. 'Anyway, how do you know this?'

'AB, Andy Bell. He was my guv, once. Eastender, talked a lot about this stuff. They get it instead of fairy tales. Maybe they are fairy tales. This place certainly is.'

I necked the half. Her drink was still full. A bottle of ersatz orange juice. She'd peeled the label off and it was in tiny pieces in front of her. When I got back from the bar, she'd shuffled around in the seat. Put some distance between us, unless I chose to fill the space. I didn't.

'So? What *is* your name?

'Grant's fine, Loan if you must.'

She riffled the confetti'd label with her fingers.

'Come on.'

It's Euphemia, Effie. A family name.'

'Scots though eh?'

'Yeah, it was my uncle's mother's name. Tell anyone and you're dead.'

'Our secret.'

She looked upward over my shoulder. I turned. Needles. Early: keen or busy. I wondered which. He looked a little less battered. Nodded at Grant, peered at her, trying to place her in his journo's universe, gave up, sat down.

'DC Grant, Needles, my journalist friend.'

'Acquaintance, The Bill don't have friends, nowadays.'

He touched the side of his nose with a finger, as if the fake geezer atmosphere was catching.

'Getting my own then?' He said.

'What do you want?' Grant stood.

'Malt, not a crap one. Tell the Barman it's for me.'

She left.

Needles jerked his head after her. 'Who's that?'

'I told you.'

'Yeah... you did. What is it then? I am busy.'

I told him the ForSec was implicated, but probably not culpable in the PM's death; I told him the circumstances were embarrassing, know-what-I-mean, for the government. I told him I still couldn't understand the business with the HomSec, Kilgour. Why had he deliberately got himself nicked? Needles gave a satisfied

'Aaaah.'

'What?'

'So that's it then. It's not a story yet, is it? I admit it - 20 years ago I'd have run to the redtops and named my price. But no-one would touch it now.'

'Yeah, but... don't you miss investigative reporting?'

He laughed, a dying cough deep in his throat.

'Look, really, I am interested. It's just... there is something going on.'

'What do you mean?'

'Pick up a paper, any of them. It's after 12, you'll get one now.'

'So what? Come on give.'

'The front pages. It's what's on them.'

'Southall? The Army?'

'Exactly. Don't know what happened at other papers, but the Standard got a visit from a creepy guy with a Home Office ID. We had the PM on the front page...

fuck all detail, less than was on the TV.'

'He told you to get the PM off the front page?'

'Not at all. He said he'd like to see Southall on it. Gave me a number to get an army escort in and out. Said he expected full and frank coverage. Oh, and he gave me a password...'

'Smokescreen.' Grant and I said. She put his malt in front of him.

'So, that's why I'm busy. I'm going back. Embedding with an Army unit in the Enclave. Report anything tonight.'

'Don't.'

'Why?'

'Try Chinatown instead. You won't have an Army minder though.'

'I can look after myself.' He touched a fading bruise on his cheekbone.

'I hope so.'

Grant and I stood. She was half-way to the door and Needles tugged my sleeve:

'I know who she is.

'I know, I told you.'

'No,' he hissed.

'That's Kilgour's niece. The HomSec's niece. Only relative, not married is he?'

I shrugged his hand off my sleeve, left the Hat and Beggar and the not-quite 1960's behind.

In the Mini, the beep of my mobile broke the silence.

'13.00. SOCO to Cabinet Office at 14.00.'

Off-Cut went up a notch or two in my estimation: as did the day's mobile service. SMS delivery in 15 minutes: fast. Another beep: another message. I'd look at it later.

The SOCO team were already there. Two sexless white-suited figures had their back to us. Bent over a corner of the long cabinet office table. I cleared my throat.

They turned: a male female team. I knew the woman; it was Yolanda's sister, Jean Okocha.

'Weren't you told to wait for us?'

'Didn't know it was you, Ray.'

'How long have you been here?'

'20 minutes. There's nothing here for you anyway, Ray.'

The guy with her took a turn clearing his throat. Jean gave him a look:

'Yeah, OK. You should know that the table is clean of all biological forensic and has been

repaired. All six chairs at this end are showroom new.'

I turned to Grant;

'I've left my mobile in the car, get it, would you?'

I darted a look at her guy. Jean said:

'Get the other camera from the van.'

I waited. So did Jean. We both started to talk at once. Then she deferred to me:

'Why are you looking at the furniture?'

'Your team told us to. We got a second call, telling us what to look at.'

'Get a name?'

'No. I didn't.' She snapped. 'Listen. It's tomorrow.'

'What?'

'The flight. They're leaving. Your family? My sister.'

'Thanks.'

Grant came in, looking flustered and perhaps a little annoyed:

'I can't find it, your mobile.'

'Doesn't matter.' I waggled the phone at her. 'We're finished here, anyway.'

Jean contaminated the sanitised crime scene with her saliva, a foot away from my shoes. We went back to the Task Force HQ.

Chapter 14

"One day you might die laughing"

It was a little after three. No sign of the Thompson Twins. Good; I felt uncomfortable around them. I sat at my desk. Maybe I should just follow the tug of the strings, I certainly didn't know my next move. The phone rang.

'DI Murray speaking.'

'ACC Pressley, afternoon Murray.'

'What can I do for you sir?'

'DS DuToit is to be stood down from duty at 1700, Murray. Do I make myself clear?'

'Swarovski, sir, Swarovski.'

'You're so funny, Murray. One day you might die laughing.'

He hung up. I'd provoked him into a threat. That was funny.

SMOKESCREEN

Fritz the Twat wasn't. He had a bag slung over his shoulder and blew me a kiss from the doorway. Then he put a finger to the corner of each eye and pulled his eye-lids taut. Twat by name.

I folded my arms on the desk, rested my head. I could see Off-Cut's belly on the other side.

'What?' I said to his navel.

'Uhmm, who's duty dog tonight, if it's not Fritz?'

'Why? Got a hot date?'

'No... my mum's sick.'

'Go on, fuck off then. I'll be here all night, anyway.'

My mouth tasted like... like it deserved to. The problem with Guinness is it coats the tongue with a fur the colour of the head on a pint of it. Pity it doesn't have

the same taste.

'Awake then?'

Grant still looked like that improbable woman copper from that 80's thing: Dempsey or Makepiece, whichever one it was.

'You got a wardrobe in the Ladies'? I croaked.

'I keep a suitcase in the car.'

'And an iron.'

She tutted:

'You could do with a shower, you

know.'

'Because my best friend won't tell me?'

'I mean, it. You look bad. You might need to be taken seriously, some time.'

'I don't think so; I think somebody reckons I'm ideal casting for my part.'

'Well, Guv, you fucking stink! And you'll feel better, really.'

'Are you my mother? Alright...Alright! Where will I get an effing shower though?'

'Go through the bar, a door at the back of the stockroom. There's a shower and lav in there. It's supposed to be for the staff. Some of the members use it to
wash off the evidence, if late night discussions get too...heated.'

'Who told you that?' I asked, but she didn't answer.

She'd been right. I did feel better. I felt like a drink. Grant was on my phone. She waved me over. Mouthed 'McCrackers' at me.

'I'll hand you over, sir'

I took the phone.

'Murray.'

'Listen, you focker, I want to know what's going on.'

'So do I, sir, so do I.'

'Ye're a cheeky bastard, all right! Well, what about it?'

'Not on the phone, sir. And I'm stuck here 'til 8 tomorrow.'

'I'll come there. Just you, is it?'

'Me and DC Grant. I'll get the sherry out.'

'Oh,you are a fonny focker!' His handset crashed down.

Grant was coming towards me brandishing some crumpled newsprint.

'Front page of the Standard. Found it on the floor of the Ladies.'

'Where's the rest of it?'

'Don't ask.'

'Wait a minute, who else has been in there apart from you?'

'Elvis' driver?' She offered; her lip trembling, voice cracking.

'What's up?'

'Nothing.' But something was.

The mirror in the ladies was smeared. Some of the newsprint had marked the glass, but not as much as what was causing the smell. The rest of the Standard had blocked one of the toilets, a steady rivulet rode the pedestal's contours before puddling inkily on the tiles.

'What did it say?' I asked Grant.

'Usual shit' She gave a snotty laugh, wiped her upper lip with the back of her hand. 'Sorry about that.'

'Don't worry about it. But you'd better tell me.'

'They'd written in ... you know.'

She retched suddenly, dry heaves. I guessed she'd already emptied her guts.

'What did it say?'

'Choose your side. Blood is thicker...' She darted a look at me. 'You know don't you.'

'Needles knows everyone in Politics.'

'It's not how it looks.'

'Isn't it? How is it then?'

'He didn't even know I was on the team, until he was here.'

I guffawed, started coughing. Grant whacked me on the back. I flung out an arm, not caring what it connected with. She backed off, lucky this

time.

'Oh he's a cool customer, Uncle Macaulay, isn't he?' I sputtered.

'I haven't even spoken to him.'

Her bottom lip came out; like a spoiled child - of 32.

'Don't you think it's odd that he hasn't spoken to you? Not even hello?'

'He's the Home Secretary! I don't know.'

And it was clear she didn't, and that it had bugged her. We spread the distressed paper on my desk, 'Elvis on the Moon' font size. Predictable 'London's Burning' headline. A photo, genuine or faked, of a burning Sikh temple in Southall according to the caption. Maybe I'd done Fritz's louts an injustice: not *Krystallnacht* but

Amritsar. Lots of people referred to the South Asian Enclave as Southall, but in truth they meant an area that covered some of what used to be the Borough of Ealing and most of Hounslow and Hillingdon. It was zoned to a certain extent: the Sikhs and Moslems rubbed along, the friction limited to causing occasional sparks between gangs of young men with nothing better do.

The byline was Needles', "Reggie Sharpe, Political Correspondent". As if such labels mattered. There wasn't that much detail: but there was more than I expected.

Policy from the government seemed to be 'No News is Good News.' They'd finally come good on that hoary old promise to get rid of spin, by not telling anyone anything. Except now they were. Or at least they were letting others do the telling. Needles quoted an unnamed source from the Enclave warning of dire consequences in other Enclaves in Oldham, Leicester and beyond, if the Army weren't withdrawn. The Muslim Council of Great Britain promised that all

Asians would support any Sikh protest. There was no editorial or opinion content in the article at all. Several soldiers were in hospital with minor injuries, one was critical but stable. Needles said that unconfirmed reports claimed that 4 South Asian men had been killed when a Scimitar had fired a shell into a stationary vehicle. The MOD declined to comment.

I could make head nor tail of it.

'Why, Grant? Why this story? They're surely not that bothered about Jackie Carlton's bit of intense briefing with the late PM? What the fuck's going on?'

But she didn't answer, she'd turned the paper over. Her finger hovered over a 2 inch square end-of-column item; 'church lead stolen' size font.

'UK refuses offer of re-entry into European Union.'

'I think it's this.'

She waggled the finger at the paragraph. She read it out:

'"Jackie Carlton said in Parliament today; '"The PM revealed to me shortly before his untimely death that he felt a headlong rush into re-union with Europe was ill-advised at this time. We do not rule out a referendum in the near future."' They don't rule it in either.'

'They know how the vote would go anyway.' I said.

'Do they?'

'Let's see. One; you can smoke. Two; you can afford to. Three; You don't have to be in Government to own a car less than ten years old. Four: the

electricity stays on all night...'

'Alright, you made your point. Only they don't. Don't know I mean. Uncle Mac says the polls are unreliable; no-one tells the truth to someone with a questionnaire and a pen any more.'

'And why is that, hey?... Uncle Mac... Jesus!'

I shook my head and walked over to the bar. Poured a Guinness. It was 10 pm. Time for some news. The TV went on. The talking head was a slickly plastic woman; Needles reckoned they called her the Token in the BBC Newsroom.

'Reports continue to come in of rioting in Chinatown in London this evening. A car was allegedly driven through the window of Won

Key's in the heart of London's
Chinatown. According to our reporter on the spot in nearby Soho, retailiatory attacks have taken place on bars and restaurants between Greek Street and Old Compton Street. We go live now to our reporter Gerry Taggart in Berwick Street outside a gentleman's club....

Some flabby mike-jockey in a flak-jacket stood next to a clearly angry Demi Chryssipous:

'Mr Chryssipous, we are standing outside your Number One Club here on Berwick Street in the aftermath of an attack on the building ...

It *was* live too. Demi interrupted:

'Some kids threw stones, bricks and one Molotov. And then they ran away.'

'Yes, quite. How do you feel about this... this...'

Definitely live; the reporter couldn't think quickly enough for Demi, who said:

'Unfortunate incident? How do I feel? Worried for the kids.'

'Why is that Mr. Christoforos?'

Demi ignored the reporter's ignorance of his name:

'I'm worried because of the people who were chasing them. They had police batons. No uniforms mind. Maybe it was a bit of community policing.'

The live feed vanished. Miss Plastic smiled nervously and explained there were 'technical problems.'

I turned the TV off.

'Still nervous, though, aren't they?'

'Who? The government?' She scrunched her lips and frowned.

'No, the journos. They yanked that pretty quick.'

'Get censored long enough and you censor yourself.'

'Very gnomic.' I thought Needles would be proud I paid so much attention.

I sat at my desk and rearranged the files for something to do. Grant seemed happy to be left with her conscience. Every so often I caught sight of her out of
the corner of my eye: rubbing her hands, dry-washing them, trying to get rid of lingering news-print or worse.

McCrackers bowled in at midnight: Barbour flapping behind him, mad-eye swivelling, hair in socketed-fingers mode:

'Murray? That Grant, is it now?'

'DC Grant, sir, yes.'

She'd taken a liking to her field-promotion. Pity it was only me who'd conferred it on her.

'What can I do for you, sir?' I asked.

The eye settled down a little.

'A report. Make an old man happy.'

I told him: just an outline; just Prime Minister stuff, not the rest. He laughed out loud at the thought of the PM's knob being the death of him. I thought he would lose interest, once he realised there had been no murder. Once again I'd underestimated him, or his hatred of Elvis.

'So what's all the fuss about then? Why the pantomime? Elvis wouldn't have come anywhere near this, unless there was something in it for him. Political
capital, I mean.'

It was the longest I'd heard him speak without swearing. Grant looked peculiar. Pale under her light tan. Something up with her, definitely.

'You OK, Grant?' #

McCrackers sounded almost concerned, and not too frightening.

She sniffed. 'Yes sir. Just something happened. This evening...'

McCrackers turned on me. He looked like his head would explode:

'What have yew donn yew FOCKIN FOCKED-UP FOCKER!'

I wiped the spittle from my face:

'Not me sir, take a look in the Ladies.'

He did. The noise was incredible. Grant and I looked at each other as we heard the cubicles' partitioning splinter and the porcelain and glassware smash. Suddenly the profanity stopped. And McCrackers' came out chest heaving. He looked on course for a medical pension, before he'd collect his retirement. He sat in one of the tubular steel chairs, shaking his head:

'That focker Elvis. That Shit Eater. It's just not...'

I brought over a drink from the bar; an amontillado bottle from a shelf. He grabbed it blindly, took a long swig. Breathed out:

'It's just not civilised.' He gathered himself, then began:

'Let me tell you about me and Elvis, and how he got his old nickname, when we got our first posting in uniform, after Hendon.'

He took another drink, loosened the military-looking tie with the tiny RUC pin holding it to his shirt:

'We both passed out of Hendon in 1980. Northholt we got. Quiet, big Polish community, not as big as now, of course. They were pleased to get us. Best two recruits of the intake. I hated him, right from the beginning. Irish jokes, 'bog-trotter' called across the canteen. I held him off for best recruit. It was the second last time I got the best of him. The Provisional IRA stepped up their campaign in the 80's; branching out. Deal barracks, soldiers overseas in Germany. It was hard. I told a WPC about my Father, why I didn't join the RUC. You remember that story, Murray, eh?'

I nodded.

'It was a stupid thing to do. We broke up. Elvis found out about what I'd told her. Anyway, one night shift I came in off patrol. Found Elvis in front of my locker. It was open. His trousers were down. Not proud of it; not now. I rubbed his nose in it, like a dog. A few others from the watch came in. It paid even then to have a certain reputation. They walked back out. You can guess his nickname, hmm? It suited him, he was a creep then and he's a creep now. I think he's got problems... almost as many as me, maybe?'

He stopped, exhausted by the story as much as the rage in the lavatories. Grant looked at me. Surprised by McCrackers' sudden withdrawal; the man's rocking motion was slight, but it was there. I shook my head. Grant and I moved to the bar.

'There's not much to do but talk now, until 'lights out.' I said.

'About what?' She was back to her spiky self.

'Life, the Universe and...'

'Anything? What about your wife, then? Leaving you, huh? Can't say I'm surprised.'

'Neither can I. You got someone?'

'Not now. How long have you been in?'

'22 years this year. '93 I joined. I was 20.'

'Seen a lot of changes then, haven't you.'

'Like you wouldn't believe.'

'What's the biggest thing? The thing that changed the most.'

I thought for a few seconds.

'2010. The White Paper: Towards More Effective 21st Century Policing.'

'What? Government legislature made the biggest change?' She asked.

'I didn't say it was a change for the better.' And her eyebrows came down.

'Why's that?'

'Elvis was part of the review team. Already an ACC for 5 years. Going places.'

'What happened?'

'More effective means cheaper. The review recommended merger of forces. Promotion on transfer disappeared.
Ever wished you'd joined the Northumbrian Police? Part of National Police North now. Nottingham to Newcastle and beyond. Guess how many
jobs went?'

'I've no idea.' She scratched her cheek, regulation clear nail varnish, nails a little long. I laughed:

'Neither have I. I know one job that did go: Elvis's next one; he was in line for the top job in the City of London force. Shafted himself for once.'

'Is that why the Praetorians are so unpopular?'

'That's part of it.' I put the TV on. 'Might as well catch the bulletins before lights out.'

'What will they say? Usual anodyne stuff the press office will allow?'

'Dunno about that. 'Strange Days'.' I waggled my eyebrows.

'I hate that game. It's a teenagers' game played by middle-aged men.'

'Yeah, it's a boy thing. Like remembering the words to songs, or air guitar.'

'Or pissing high up the wall.'

She turned to the TV screen.

'- live to Oldham, with special correspondent Robin Chatterjee.'

We raised our eyebrows at each other.

'Haven't seen him in years. Thought he'd emigrated. I would have.'

'Maybe the government has forgiven him.'

Maybe they had, I thought. He looked older, I hoped he was wiser:

'- in Oldham tonight, simmering tensions are set to blow the lid off the cauldron of race relations in England.'

Grant snorted. She had a point. Why use one cliché when you could use...

'the fuse in the powder keg is the unprovoked attacks by gangs of white males on businesses in Oldham's Enclave...

I tuned him out.

'Un-be-lievable.'

'It is,' she agreed. 'How is he getting away with that?'

'No... that's not it. When did you last see a BBC News film crew outside the Metropolitan area?'

'I never thought of that... I was concentrating on what he was saying.'

'Oh that... Journalists used to talk like that all the time. You could almost tell who they worked for by what they said or wrote.'

'I know. My degree was in Language Studies.'

The Token was still on duty in the News Room. I guessed she'd be overnighting at Television Centre, what with the curfew. She changed to another item:

'Earlier tonight, we reported on retaliatory attacks by Chinatown gangs on businesses in nearby Soho. We return to Berwick Street for an interview with a Police Officer on the scene.'

Fritz the Twat's ugly mug was on the screen, Flabby Flak-Jacket held a microphone in his fat hand.

'Detective Sergeant DuToit...' Fritz winced.

Flabby went up in my estimation for carefully mispronouncing Fritz's name:

' can you brief us on the events of the last few hours in Soho and Chinatown?'

'We have made a number of arrests and the situation is calm, if tense. The Metropolitan Police appeal to all responsible members of the public

to remain calm.'

'Detective Sergeant, are there any clues as to the cause of the increase in civil disturbance over the last few days? Are events in the South Asian Enclave and those of tonight linked in any way?'

The director went tight on Fritz's face, who composed his features in what he believed was a sincere expression:

'No, and no,' he said

'Fockin' liar!'

I flinched. McCrackers that close to your ear required protection to be worn.

'Sir...' I hesitated.'How did you get through the curfew?'

'I've got some friends left in the Met, you cheeky bastard. Besides; that fockin' Smokescreen business is the dog's bollocks. I wish I'd thought of it.'

'It won't work forever.' Grant said.

'Why not?' McCrackers and I chimed.

'It's viral. The more often it's used, the more people can overhear it. I bet only a handful of people know what it actually means. But everyone can see it's effect.Think of it as, I don't know, the latest gadget, once everyone has one, it's not exclusive, is it? It's lost its value. Or... Monopoly, the game, you know.'

'What are ye talkin' about?' McCrackers held off the swearing, maybe he was intrigued.

'Well, think of it as a 'Get Out of Jail Free' card. Now, there are what, two in the Chance deck yeah? What if there were one for each player? And you didn't give it up, you kept it, used it again and again?'

'The Jail would be just another square.' I said.

'Exactly.'

McCrackers gave a harrumph worthy of a retired army Colonel.

'I'm getting my head down. One of youse wake me up before the day shift comes in. I don't want to run into anyone else.'

I grabbed a malt and sat on one of the banquettes, wondering which flight my wife and daughter were leaving on.

Chapter 15

"We're going to watch democracy's inaction"

But when I woke up at 8.00 am, McCrackers was gone. Grant wasn't in sight but I heard the shower in the back going. The TV was on. Kicked in as the lights came back on, same as I had. The Thompson Twins grunted a greeting, sat down at a shared desk and powered up their laptop. Abramowicz came in about 8.30. I called him over.

'What happens to probationers, Abramowicz?'

'They get all the shit jobs, sir.' He really was intelligent.

'There's a mess to clean up in the Ladies. It's not nice and I don't want it to be gossip here or anywhere, get it?'

'Got it, sir.'

'Guv, Abramowicz. Guv.'

'Yes s-Guv.' I reckoned he might make a policeman, at that.

There was a big surprise at 9.00. Fritz and Off-Cut were still missing, George was in. Elvis arrived, but that wasn't the surprise. There was some one with him. Elvis clapped his hands for everyone's attention:

'I'd like to present a new member of the team, and ask you to congratulate Detective Inspector Aristotle Chrissypous on his recent promotion.'

There was a half-hearted round of applause, a few grunts of acknowledgement. Elvis looked particularly pleased with himself. Harry Xeno looked embarassed. I nodded at him. Elvis barked:

'Carry on, gentlemen.'

With what? I thought, as I got yet another view of his ramrod back.

Fritz and Off-Cut rolled up, deep in conversation. I shouted for attention:

'I'm sure DI Chrissypous will be a valuable addition to the team. His role will be to keep the ACC informed of developments. I expect to wrap things up today. Grant and I will be out and about in Westminster today. DS Wilton will be point of contact here.'

I had a go at the confident exit all the VIPs had been showing me over the past few days. Spoiled it by tripping over McCrackers's empty amontillado from the night before.

'Are we really hanging round here all day?' Grant groaned.

'Yep, we're going to watch democracy's inaction.'

'Don't you mean... ha, ha. Very funny.'

The security check to get into the Strangers' Gallery was thorough. A female Praetorian with the company haircut gave Grant the treatment behind a modesty partition. She didn't have any purple powder bombs hidden about her person. We'd shown our warrant cards, but it had made no difference. I resisted the temptation of 'Smokescreen.' Better to save it for when there was something to hide.

We were sitting in the Gallery. The Members had 'dough-nutted' the front benches for the TV cameras; making sure it looked like the house was full. The 'Opposition' was a misnomer; there wasn't any. Off-message MPs
from the only party were banished to the other side of the house, where they quickly learned any serious effort at opposing meant an even longer stay there.

'What are we doing here, Guv?

'Call me, Ray.'

'Well what, Ray?'

'I thought we'd visit Uncle Mac at work.'

'I told you: he didn't know.'

House business, superficially, continued as it always had: early day motions, filibusters, PM's Questions – pro-tem PM's questions that week. In about 2 hours. Kilgour was due to give a statement on the civil disturbances before that. His first appearance in the House, since the PM's death.

'Uncle Mac, Scottish Parliament, wasn't he?'

'Yeah...'

'One of the rats, huh?'

'What's that supposed to mean?' Her eyes narrowed.

'Let's just say he saw the Iceberg coming.'

'The Scottish Parliament was a brave experiment. If Westminster had kept up the subsidies...'

'Come on! I'm a Jock. Even the most rabid Nationalist realised we couldn't spend money we didn't have, in the end.'

'I didn't know you were a student of Politics.' She tugged at the hem of her skirt.

'I'm not,' I said. 'I just wish we'd been a bit less successful on the devolution thing.'

'It's still the United Kingdom.'

I laughed. Pointed down at the front benches. Kilgour was on his feet.

'All hail the Once and Future King!'

'Foreign Secretary, Mr Speaker, Honourable Members...'

I looked at Grant; her mouth was slightly open, eyes wide, fixed on Uncle Mac. I watched her pupils dilating. I thought I'd ask her about Kilgour's speech afterwards. It would be better than a tape-recording. The Home Secretary was confident, very occasional looks down at credit card sized notes. The posh Jock accent held more than Grant spellbound. The words themselves... well, political speeches... 'parvum in multo' as a superannuated teacher had written on one of my school essays. Latin he said it was. Told me it meant 'Little in Much.' He was an odd fish, even for a teacher. The nub of Kilgour's speech was that 'it might be necessary for the many to sacrifice some liberty in the cause of overall freedom.'

I thought of something else that teacher had written on another piece of work: 'Plus ça change.'

There was another hour to go before Jackie Carlton took PM's questions. Someone had asked the Speaker's permission to rebut. It made me think of cigarettes. But he just stood up and tried to sound like he was disagreeing, but didn't. Now that Kilgour had sat down, Grant had lost the Stepford Wife look.

'Good speech that.'

'You think so?' Grant put her hand on my thigh.

'Oh yes. Only lasted an hour. Some of these buggers can drivel for England. Or Scotland, come to that.' The hand was withdrawn.

'He's so... Charismatic.'

'Like Hitler.' I said.

'Are we done here?' She tutted.

'No, we're going to listen to the PM pro-tem. And when they take the comfort break, we're going to abuse our position as members of the Constabulary and talk

to the woman in question.'

'You really are fucking mad, aren't you?'

But she was fighting to keep the corners of her mouth down.

'First I've got to go outside.' I said.

'Why?'

'Need to use my mobile; I'll have to get a Praetorian to check the phone out and stand next to me while I use it, won't I? Are you sure you're

related to Kilgour?'

'Never had to use mine here.'

We only had to wait 25 minutes for the break. There were a lot of old people in the house nowadays.

'Back in 5.'

It took 10 minutes of cajoling to persuade the Praetorian woman that 5 minutes of her time was worth my mobile phone use. She looked mortified as I thumbed an SMS:

'12.15.Yol, please give me the flight number and time. For Vicky's sake, please.'

'Wait. I need to read it.'

'It's private.'

'Come on, you know the score.' She read it; I sent it.

Grant had gone zombified again. Kilgour was on his feet once more; replying to the non-rebuttal. I hoped I'd been in time with the text message. Saying goodbye to my daughter seemed so much more important than the

charade of the investigation. I wouldn't get a reply. The chamber was TEMPEST sealed. Nothing could get through; microwave, radio-wave, maybe even tidal wave. TEMPEST had been developed for the Military and GCHQ; no signals out – and more importantly for a terrorist target like Parliament- no signals in.

Kilgour, charisma or no, drivelled to a halt, by design perhaps. I watched him pass Carlton a file. Punched her shoulder in as false a gesture of bonhomie-ous encouragement as I ever hoped to see. The BBC still filmed all of it; although the BBC Parliament Satellite Channel was long gone. Jackie Carlton stood. She was slightly stooped, the coiffeur was still less than perfect: I thought she looked older.

'I would ask the Honourable Prime Minister Pro Tem what steps are being taken to resolve the leadership question? Are we, and the nation, to continue in limbo...'

It was the Windbag: still able to function without his inalienable right to the Commons Bar. I wondered if Carlton would remember what the question was by the time the hot air shut off.

She did: 'We ask the honourable member for...'

For I still didn't care where. Carlton asked for patience at this difficult time. Said the Police hadn't finished with their enquiries. Promised a resolution to the Leadership question as soon as 'feasible.' Which was as meaningless a time-frame as I could imagine. There was another question: how long would the Army be on the streets? She might have looked rough, but her replies were as non-commital as they were rehearsed. Still a politician.

Windbag stood again:

'Would the PM Pro Tem please inform the house as to her knowledge of events surrounding the late Prime Minister's death?'

Pandemonium: all the demons out, yelling, catcalls, the Speaker's gavel, shouts of 'Order! Order! Kilgour smiled enigmatically throughout; finally holding up one finger in the Speaker's eyeline. Order restored, the Speaker called for a comfort break; another break with tradition – Members had to hold their water until the end of Prime Minister's Questions as a rule, after the customary single break. The Members trooped out. Carlton and Kilgour were deep in conversation.

'Let's go. The lobby.' Grant and I left at a run.

Kilgour didn't seem surprised to see us. Carlton seemed beyond all emotion. The lobby was full; the whispers of the MPs trying to recall a similar breach of protocol.

'Uh.. is it Prime Minister, or what?' I asked, holding up my warrant card.

'Yes... Inspector, is it?' She squinted at the ID.

'The Inspector is head of the Task Force investigating the late PM's death.'

Kilgour explained.

'Oh. I'm not sure how I can help you, Inspector.'

I turned to Kilgour:

'Home Secretary, if my colleague and I might speak with the PM alone?'

His mouth tightened to a thin line.

"Of course. Jackie, I'll be...' He waved airily towards a corner.

Grant watched him all the way. I clicked my fingers in front of her eyes. There was a tut from Jackie Carlton. Perhaps there was still life in the old girl yet.

'Prime Minister,' I began.

'Call me Jackie.'

It was automatic: had been since Blair. Meant nothing then; meant nothing now.

'I'd rather not, Prime Minister. I'll get to the point. We have some video...'

'Yes, yes, the body was moved, I know that.'

That's not what's on this video.'

Her hand went to her mouth; her face didn't quite go the green of the seat she'd been sitting on a few minutes ago; but it was close. Grant grabbed her arm, held her upright. Carlton began waving frantically at Kilgour, who gave that smile before composing himself and running over.

'Ok, Jackie. I'll deal with this.'

He signalled a minor member of the Cabinet; Agriculture, or something. Side parting, uncertain teeth. Who cared what their names were anyway? Minor Member took the PM over to a drinks fountain.

'Look, I know what you have. You know it means nothing. There has been no crime, Murray.'

'Actually, you're wrong.'

'What? It was an accident.'

'There was still a crime. It's against the law to die in Parliament.'

'You know the video's from the Cabinet Office.'

'It's the TOD, sir, the Time of Death; there's a blood gases report and a couple of other things to come. Are you sure he was quite dead, when you and the then Foreign
Secretary moved him?'

'Yes, of course I'm sure! I check-...'

He checked himself as it dawned on him what he'd said.

'Thank you, sir. I'll be making my report this evening.'

Kilgour turned on his heel. Grant was looking as his feet as he walked away, checking for traces of clay on the carpet.

Chapter 16

"Ever read Le Carre?"

We were outside, in the car park.

'I'm going to have a kip, Grant. Give us your car keys.'

'Nah, I'll sit in the car and keep an eye on you. You can have half an hour, Guv.'

'Oh can I?' I checked for the bottle in my jacket pocket. Sat in the passenger seat. Slept.

Grant was shaking me seconds later. Or it seemed like it.

'You got three-quarters. Two messages came in on your phone.'

'When?' I fumbled in my pockets.

'Just.' She handed me my phone.

'Fingers Grant? Could have been a dip.' I smiled at her.

'Uncle Mac taught us magic tricks, when we were small. It's the same skills.'

Us? I thought. I brought up the first SMS: said to Grant;

'Guess what? Elvis wants us. At Task Force HQ.'

'Better go then, eh?'

'Not likely; there's got to be some advantages to the crap service we get from the mobile companies.'

'What's the second message?'

I looked at it.

'12.15. Border Guards 1400 Check in 1500.' Boarding 1700. Come and say goodbye to Vicky... Please.'

'What's it say, Guv?'

'It says you'd better take me to Heathrow.'

We made good time, in spite of having to go around the Enclave. We arrived at the Border Guards' checkpoint on the perimeter fence at 1530. Check 'point' didn't
quite convey the vast ranks of...well, it looked like the entry to a French Toll road. 20 booths 20 barriers, cars 10 deep at each one. I looked over at Grant. She looked pissed off:

'Hey, ever read Le Carre?' She asked me.

'What? Yes, something about a Looking Glass. Old hat that stuff, Cold War.'

'I was just thinking: the heroes in those books: always trying escape the Border Guards.'

'"People's Border Guards": watch out for anything with "People's" in the name.'

'Yeah... anyway, they were always trying to get out. Remember when they set this lot up?'

'What about it?'

'They were supposed to stop people getting in.'

She laughed, a soft sigh of a laugh. It was the saddest thing I'd ever heard.

At the front of the queue it was a struggle;

'ID' One of the guards, flat-faced, surly.

'Police.' I held up a warrant card.

'Flight Tickets.' Flat estuarine vowels.

'Police, I said.'

'No Tickets, no entry.'

His partner hefted the Heckler and Koch, moved it out of 'port' position. I hoped he wasn't going to go Brazilian on us.

'Call the supervisor, eh? It is Police Business.'

'Ok, through the barrier. Pull off to the left into the bay.'

We did. The closed sign went up on this lane. I could almost hear the swearing and sighs from the queue.

'Out.' He made a flat, sweeping motion with his hand.

We stood over to the side as ordered. Two unarmed uniforms arrived. They took the car to pieces. I felt embarassed for Grant as Flat Face took personal responsibility for Grant's case of clothes.

'Why have you got a case if you're not going anywhere?' he asked me.

'It's not my case.' I said.

'You never know.'

I didn't punch him because Grant leaned towards him and said:

'It's mine, and I'm moving in with him tonight. I'm not surprised you didn't recognise female clothing. Now where is that supervisor?'

'When we've finished.'

And when they had, they said 'carry on'. We put the hubcaps back on, put the spare back in: Grant repacked the clothes in her case, in spite of the dirt smeared on them by the damp tarmac. It was 4.15. Grant dropped me at the bus-stop on the way to the car park. The bus ride took 10 minutes. I took the terminal-link monorail to the newest and last terminal.

In the departures hall I heard the tannoy:

'Passengers Ms Yolanda Okocha-Murray and Miss Victoria Okocha-Murray please go to boarding gate 37b.'

That was early. I hoped there wasn't a problem, for Yol's sake. I ran to the Air Nigeria desk. Prayed she would be hanging around. She wasn't.

My daughter Vicky and my wife were nearing the front of the snake to final security. I waved frantically. Yolanda caught my eye. Turned Vicky towards her, put her arms around her, preventing her from seeing me. And then they were gone. Airside. And nowadays, once you were airside, you had effectively left the country. I took the bottle out of my pocket; a 25 cl bottle of Red Wine nicked from the Commons Bar. Just like the ones you bought on aeroplanes. It tasted good on the way down.

Grant found me in one of the bars, an hour later. I was in conversation with a Russian businessman; he'd told me he'd stayed as long as he could, for his daughter's education. His family had gone; he'd sold up. Paris first, then somewhere – anywhere – else. I wished him luck. He'd bought the drinks, after all.

'You sober?' Grant asked.

'Should I be?'

'Well, we'd better go meet Elvis, see what he wants.'

'What do you think he wants?'

'Reports, updates. Maybe the whole thing wrapped up.'

'I don't think so. This thing's been wrapped since before we came on the scene.'

'Only one way to find out.'

Chapter 17

No Suspicious Circumstances

The 'Murder Wall' was gone: the laptops too. No-one had mentioned the missing one. Details. Fritz was lounging against the bar, Off-Cut was on a stool trying to even up the height difference. No sign of the rest of the team. Then Harry Xeno's head appeared from behind the Gents' door;

'Ray, here. The ACC wants a word.'

I set off for the lavs; Grant started to follow, I raised my eyebrows at her. She shrugged and went to sit at the bar, as far away from Fritz as possible. Elvis wiped his nose with the back of his hand. Sniffed.

'Bad cold?' I said.

'I warned you about that humour.' He flicked a glance at Harry, who punched me in the nuts.

'Messy.' Elvis said, as he stepped gingerly away from my pool of vomit.

'Right. Your report is on your desk. All you have to do is sign it.'

'What did I write?'

I was still on the floor. Harry was ok, his kick landed in my ribs, not my balls.

'What do you think? Tragic unexplained accident, no suspicious circumstances, we may never know what really happened.'

One of the cubicles was showing 'engaged'. I couldn't see the feet, there was a bag,and a coat was visible too.

'Don't the public have a right to know what really happened?'

Elvis sniggered; 'The Public: the People's right-to-know.

'I want the video,' he went on.

'I haven't got it.'

'Come on, don't be stupid.' The voice was lighter, less harsh.

'It's at the bottom of the Thames. It was on a Smart Card, in a laptop.'

'Anyone else seen it?'

'No.'

'I wouldn't have thought your computer skills were up to that.'

'It was easy. Anyone could do it. Except maybe you, Harry.'

He gave me another kick. A good egg, Harry, on the knee this time.

'Anyway, Murray, that means you're the only loose end.'

He looked at Harry Xeno, who banged on the cubicle door.

Yolanda and Vicky stepped over the bag and coat;

'Ray, what the hell have you done now?' Yol said.

'Get up, Daddy. It's dirty down there,' said Vicky.

'Let them go.' Yeah, I pleaded.

'Outside, certainly. They can wait in the bar. DI Chryssipous?'

Harry took them out. Vicky was happy to take Uncle Harry's hand. Yol wasn't happy that he took her arm. I got up, Elvis watched me struggle. I looked at him. The creases at the side of his mouth deep. His blue eyes were unreadable, the pupils dilated, glittering.

'They were air-side, I saw them.'

'We can do anything. We're strong, this country needs strong people, a strong leader.' The words sounded familiar.

'What now?' I asked him.

'Well, we're not unreasonable people. You sign the report, make the press statements. Your wife and child leave. Who knows, you cooperate, maybe you could
leave too? In a couple of months when everything's in place...'

'What do you mean?'

'When everything's in place? It won't matter, you won't matter. D'you see?'

I didn't. But he saw something, A vision. Maybe that's how he saw himself, as a visionary. Uniformed visionaries. Always dangerous. But what could I do?

'OK, I'll do it,' I said.

And because I'd asked Grant to stash the smart card away somewhere safe, I resolved to get that video to Needles, one day.

Chapter 18

"Police and Thieves"

The paperwork was on my desk. Yol and Vicky had gone. One had said nothing to me and I had tried to make the other understand. It would have been heartbreaking whichever way round that had been. There was a statement for me to read to the press. That was for tomorrow. My twenty fifth signature could have been anyone's, the last two I signed as Ray Mancini; my name in the Number Six. They looked the same, more or less. Only details. Grant appeared at the desk, looking over both shoulders. Everyone was gone:

'That it, then?' I wondered what she expected.

'Got the Vid? Somewhere safe?' I hoped so.

'Yeah. The Praetorians didn't find it, did they?'

She gave a superior smile. I didn't ask. It seemed a long time ago. Since we were Bill, the search hadn't been so thorough. She'd taken a chance though, if the rubber gloves had come out...

'We need copies and we need to put them somewhere safer than safe.'

'What for, it's not important, is it?'

'I think it is, at least for a while.' I let her think about that.

My desk was the last trace of 'Task Force HQ'. Under my press statement, was a note from Elvis.

'Don't fuck up. At the station by 10 tomorrow. Ready for the cameras.'

It wasn't signed. But he'd used his headed notepaper again. Perhaps my former partner carried it about for him, now.

'Copies, Grant, where?' I looked up at Grant again, in fact I didn't have a clue about this stuff, despite what I'd told Elvis.

'Loads of places. But... we want untraceable, no questions asked copies, eh?'

'So?'

'We need a geekster, you know, one of the gangs' pet IT freaks.'

'They've got computer experts?'

'Jeez... When was the last time you did some police work, Guv? Other than rough up a potential suspect, that is?'

I didn't care to answer that.

The Number Six was crowded. I saw Harry Xeno over in a corner, with Fritz and Off-Cut. They weren't smokers. Harry looked away, when I caught his eye. Grant and I shoehorned ourselves in at the bar. A biggish guy turned rapidly on Grant; did a double take, then checked her out. Liked what he saw, by the look of it.

'Quite finished? Did I pass?' she smiled sweetly at him.

'Yeah, you passed alright.' He gave another leer for luck.

'You didn't though. Fuck off.' And she turned her back on him. The guy tapped his temple over her shoulder at me. I gave him a discreet finger.

Woodbine got to us after a few minutes:

'What do you want?'

'Drinks first.'

'So, what d'you want?'

'I'll have the unusual, Grant'll have a Virgin Mary.'

'Be unusual if I gave that to you,eh?'

But he didn't; he just gave me the usual 'unusual': the first drink that came into his head. I'd ordered the 'unusual' in memory of my friendship with Harry Xeno, with whom I'd 'unusualled' myself into oblivion several times. The drinks arrived and mine looked like Jekyll's potion with added fruit. Tasted better than it looked, though that was probably the alcohol. I paid Woodbine straight away. He nodded and said:

'I'll get back to you. When it's quieter.'

'What's all that about?' Grant wanted to know.

'I always run a tab here. If I pay him immediately he knows there's something else: business.'

'Cute.' She nodded, agreeing with her own assessment.

'Careful,' I said, and set about turning into Mr Hyde.

A couple of hours later, as Woodbine passed us again on the way to the Guinness tap. I held a hand up to stop him. He turned, bared his teeth;

'What? Told you I'd get to you later. What you tink?'

'No, it's important. Those guys with Harry Xeno...'

He interrupted: 'With Chryssipous?

I must have looked surprised:

'Come on, you really tink your stupid smoker's names fool anyone? We are in business here, illegal business. We need to know who we deal with.'

'Fair enough, but –' I felt brave. 'But you can talk; Carlton Woodbine.' I snorted

'It's my real name... Almost. It's Charlton, Charlton Woodbine. It was a school thing. It stuck.'

I kept a straight face, just: 'Harry - Ari's - friends. Been here before?'

'No. I recognise that big South African, I see him before, not here though, mon.'

'He's from Namibia. Fritz the Twat. Been on the telly recently.'

'They all sound the same to me.' Woodbine said.

'Listen, watch out for trouble, next few days. Fritz is involved in some funny business. They'd like to target somewhere like this.'

'Don't they like smokers, then?'

'I'm afraid it's not that.' I said.

He gave a slow nod : 'Thanks, Ray. '

Grant stared after him:

'Where's he from?'

'Kingston, Jamaica.'

'Bollocks, he is.'

'His parents are.

'Maybe, but that Yardie talk is bolted on. A few tanks and tinks and the odd mon don't make him a Yardie. He even forgets to do it, sometimes.'

'Where is he from, then?'

'Dunno, but I know what kind of school he went to.'

'How?'

'Vowels, Ray.'

'Same to you.' I took a drink, she persisted in educating me.

'Take yours for example; I put you from Glasgow, although you're smoothed down by English living. Probably since you were around 15.'

'What about him?' I pointed at Woodbine, he noticed.

'Put it this way: the skeleton in his closet is wearing the old school tie.'

I thought about that for a few seconds. We both started to laugh at the same time. The hysterical, unstoppable laughter that comes from being over-tired and stressed out; the kind that even the lamest joke that wouldn't raise a titter at midday can provoke towards midnight. A pointlessly telepathic moment; we were both wondering whose fag 'Carlton Woodbine' had been at school. I'd almost recovered. Grant gave me a wide-eyed look. Woodbine was back;

'What's so funny, Ray?' The reasonable, cultured voice of a vicar.

I was about to tell him, Grant gave me a kick from a pointy, useless for police-work shoe: she leapt in:

'What's the name of the Foreign Secretary, Mr Woodbine?'

'What is this? An audition for a TV quiz show?'

'No, seriously.' She beamed at him: full Kilgour power and there was no doubt whose niece she was. Woodbine made a pretence of thinking.

'Carlton. They call her Jackie, but that's not her name. Some mix up about footballers, by Blair, that it?'

'Well... you went from Charlton to Carlton. She almost went the other way.'

'Huh. I'll talk to you later, like I said.'

Woodbine drew up to his full height, slapped an evil-looking cloth into the pool of drink I'd spilled. Spread it out in front of me, flicked some drops at me on lifting the cloth. Public School or not, he was a very scary man.

Harry Xeno and his new pals had left during our giggling fit. So had most of the other smokers. Breaking the curfew with impunity; I wondered where in the city it was being enforced. It would be an easy guess. It wasn't midnight in fact, it was only just 11. The smoke was curling up towards the ceiling, the air was clearing at eye-level. Grant was looking at me; I tried not to think about what she saw. I picked at something unidentifiably crusty on my trousers at the top of my thigh. Sometimes I wasn't sure if I was plummeting to the bottom, or it was hurtling upwards towards me.

I signalled for a drink; Woodbine crashed a Long Island Iced Tea onto the bar in front of me, a stain began to cover the unidentified crust:

'What you want?' His arms were folded, the chin was out.

'Help. We need you to copy something, and we need you to keep it for us.'

'Copy?'

'A disc, smart card thing. It has information on it. Important information.'

'How I do that, mon? You see any computers in here?'

Grant rolled her eyes: 'Come on, you don't live on the proceeds from this dive!'

Woodbine turned his head, slowly, as stiff necked as a robot:

'Maybe I don't. So what?'

'So you have someone who can do it, that's all.'

He grunted. Then: 'What's in it for me?'

'Fritz, Fritz the Twat, from earlier? He's involved in the disturbances in the Enclave and Chinatown.'

'Policing them?'

Although I thought he already knew the answer to that, I said: 'Not really.'

He put his hands on the bar and leaned forward.

'You keep me posted, on this stuff?'

'Of course.' I wasn't convinced I'd be able to do that.

'Deal.' He held out a hand. I shook it, ignored the strange grip. He nodded, then shrugged.

'One more thing.' Grant 'Kilgour-ed' him with the smile again. Her reward was the corner-twitched mouth:

'What?'

'We'll need to stay here, tonight.'

'The bar's yours, once the last customer's gone. I'll be in the stock-room.'

I said 'Thanks.' But I was talking to his back as he went to the other end of the bar.

As Woodbine pulled down the shutters on the bar, I sat on the floor, back against the bar; Grant retreated to a sort of booth in one corner. I lit up and waited for sleep.

The shakes started as soon as I woke up. The juke box came on when the power did. Woodbine laughed:

'It always does that. Better than an alarm clock.'

It looked like he hadn't needed it. Grant was probably sorting through her case for some clean clothes. I sorted through my pockets for a cig.

'Is it always the same record?' I asked.

'No, you're just lucky today, recognise it do you?'

'I think so... What is it?'

He gave a massive grin. Old Stoneface himself cracked a beamer of a smile:

'It's very old, 70's, Junior Murvin...' He paused. 'It's called Police and Thieves.'

Chapter 19

"We're playing 'Spies'"

Grant and I pulled up at my nick in the mini. Two hubcaps gone, it was a shame. I'd put them on at the Border Guards checkpoint. She didn't say anything. Patel was on again. Unpaid overtime or problems at home; amounted to the same thing really. He waved me over, told me the ACC was looking for me. I was clutching a file containing my police report and press statement.

'I'll go up then. Wait here Grant, OK?'

She nodded.

I nodded at DI Chryssipous, 'Harry Xeno' had passed away while I was on the floor of the Gents'. Elvis looked up from his desk.

'You're going to be sensible?'

'I've got 'my' statement.' I waved the file at him.

'Your report?'

I took the triplicates out and dropped them on the desk in front of him: 'My daughter, my wife? Where are they?'

'They're in a Border Guards office at Heathrow. Ring them, if you like, that's the number on the pad. They're under no duress; ask them anything you like.'

I picked up the phone, dialled the number. A land line, might be picked up in Heathrow. It was picked up, anyway.

'Captain Johnson.'

'I want to speak to my wife.'

'Your name.'

'DI Murray, Ray Murray.'

He covered the mouthpiece with his hand, I heard him repeat my name anyway.

'Ray. Is that you?'

'Yeah, you OK, Yol? Can you talk? '

'I think so. We're at Heathrow, stuck in some office with some military type.'

'Can I speak to Vicky?

'Look, don't upset her... we're making it a game, alright?'

'Some game.' I said.

'Daddy, Daddy.'

I swallowed: 'Hey Vick, you OK, what's the game?'

'Oh we're playing Spies.' She lowered her voice to a whisper, 'I'm only doing it for Mummy, really.'

'You're a good girl, Vick. I lov-'

Elvis grinned, his finger had severed the connection:

'Satisfied?'

'You shit-eating bastard.'

He gave me a roundhouse open-handed slap from behind his desk. Almost missed. He must have been terrified of McCrackers when they were recruits. He got control of himself, although the tips of his ears stayed red.

'Out front in half-an-hour, the BBC will be there. Make your statement. They go to Nigeria.'

'And how will I know that?'

'I expect they have phones in Nigeria too.'

What choice was there? I left his office to wait out front for the cameras.

Elvis had sent Chryssipous to keep an eye on me, maybe to step in if I deviated from the script. Grant was around out of shot. Behind the camera crew I caught sight of Needles with the other print outlet representatives. He lifted a hand about two inches in a sort of wave. I gave the statement as written. Grant caught my eye and gave a thumbs up. My former partner stepped forward and said no questions, although I guess he could have answered them, as he'd written the statement and reports. The BBC Crew dispersed and only Needles sidled round to talk some more. I shook my head, mouthed 'later' held up six fingers. It would have to do.

Grant and I went back into the Station Building. Patel said we were wanted in CID.

'Me too?' Grant asked.

'Yeah, of course.' Patel tutted.

I remembered my promise from the other day. On the way upstairs Grant said:

'But I'm not...'

'So? Walk like a duck and all that.'

'You mean...'

'Yep. No-one's going to say anything. Your pay won't change. CID gets an extra bod, who loses?' Apart from Sgt Patel, of course.

'Has this been done before??'

'What do you think?'

Ari Chryssipous was behind a brand new desk with a brand new name plate: his. I looked over at the one we used to share. One side of it was very tidy, empty. The other side was how I'd left it. Chryssipous held up a file: 'Elvis says he wants you to take this one. Another body. Your specialty, eh?'

'What is it?'

'You'll see, get over to Kilburn. Black Rose pub. Elvis says now is good.'

In the car Grant told me I smelled again. I looked up from the file: 'Not as much as this.'

'Why?'

'The body's McCrackers" I said.

Chapter 20

"The Birds Have Flown"

For once the SOCO van had turned up at the same time as us; surprisingly, Grant lost out in the game of chicken with its driver, and we had to walk further in the rain to the door of the Black Rose pub. Mill Lane was pretty much deserted, it was nearing noon and the sun was an insipid off white disc in the grey sky. The rain was fine, the kind where you're soaked in seconds without feeling a drop on your skin. The SOCO van driver slapped me hard and the expected word came out with venom. I said:

'Hi Jean. You heard?'

'Not from you, though did I? Yol got an SMS out before they took her mobile.'

'I didn't want to worry you, that's all.' And I reflected that the message hadn't come to me.

'I shan't worry *you*, in that case, shall I?' She retorted.

I caught her arm as she headed in the pub door:

'What do you know?'

'Got a call,' she shook me off, rubbed her arm. 'Captain someone or other, Border Guards.'

'Johnson?'

'Who cares? He said 'the birds have flown', kept repeating it.'

'Thank God.' I said.

But I didn't like to think about what Yol had done to get him to make that call.

Amazingly the two uniforms had kept most people out of the pub since they'd arrived. A futile effort, who knew how many people had been in and out before that.

'Jean,' I tried to get her attention, raising my voice over the crackle of her and her colleague's crime-scene coveralls. I tapped her shoulder.

'How come you got this one? Doesn't anyone else do anything?'

'It's partly that. It's a favour this one.'

'Who for?'

For answer I got a look that reminded me of many her sister had given me.

As for Grant and I there was a choice: suit up or stay out of the way. I chose the latter for both of us. We were crammed in a narrow entrance with a thin guy too old for his haircut. The entrance opened out into open plan pub with alcoves around the side. It felt like we were in a cattle chute at a slaughter house. I shoved my warrant card in the thin man's face:

'You are?'

'Deputy Bar Manager. I just opened up at 11 and there he was.'

'Barman, eh? You know him?'

'Never seen him before. Who is he?'

'How long have you worked here?' Grant was getting the hang of the Mutt and Jeff stuff.

'Three years yesterday. I had the night off.'

'Where were you?' I said.

'Old Compton Street.' He sneered it out.

'Anyone likely to confirm your whereabouts?' I put my head on one side.

'Plenty. You want twenty names? Might even be some you know.'

'Yeah... just what were you doing?.'

I put his head on one side, by the expedient of smacking the top of it as hard as I could.

'Stuff you should be doing.'

I turned to Grant:

'Get the names, I'm going out for some air.' Just one plod remained outside. Cold, wet and bored.

'Where's your mate?' I asked him.

'Comfort break.'

'I hate that. Just say he's gone for a piss, to see a man about a dog. Comfort break, my arse.'

'He's gone for a shit, sir.'

'Ok, I deserved that. Who was here when you got here?'

'Haircut.'

'No-one else?'

'Uh-uh.'

'What about out here, on the street?'

'Couple of guys. One tall, one dead short. Tall one looked familiar.'

'Didn't think to stop them, then?'

'What for? They were just walking round the corner. On their way somewhere else. They just didn't look suspicious. Could have been Bill, or anything.'

'Yeah,' I said. 'They could.'

The Police Surgeon's meat wagon arrived. One day I'd be at a death scene and everyone would turn up at once. One day. The Police Doc got out. Slowly. It was Harbottle, 'Fatty' Harbottle. He drove his own vehicle, none of the drivers Police or Civvy would do it. I tried to stay upwind of his breath:

'Murray,' he wheezed. 'What've we got?'

I looked at the sausage casing fit of his tweed and said: 'Better wait for SOCO to finish. Unless, you think they've got a coverall to fit.'

'Great, I'm off up the road to the New Alliance for a bite. Send plod when you're ready.'

He waddled off, a doctor on the point of exploding. I was dying for a cig. I went back in. To see how it was going. Grant had the thin guy by the throat.

'Modern policing, Isn't it great?' I said. She put him down.

The thin man rubbed his throat, whitening the lividity, but highlighting the scratches from the almost-regulation nails.

'Get what you wanted, Grant?'

'Almost. He gave us 18 names. He said 20.'

'That's about 20 isn't it? Leave it, you've got his details?'

'Yeah, but...'

'But bollocks. I'm getting claustrophobic. Piss off, slim!'

I gave the thin guy a helping shove out the door.

'He was hiding something, guv.' Grant made a face.

'Yeah... well, later.'

My sister-in-law and her sidekick had just about finished, if that's what the two fingers she'd showed me meant. She backed out via her own footprints in the chemicals on the dark wooden floor.

'You can have it now... If you wear overshoes. Did I hear the Doc? Who is it?'

'Fatty.' I said

'Harbottle? Oh fuck! Pie crumbs everywhere by the time he's finished. The pathologist'll never know what the last meal was, that's for sure. Ah well, it looks straightforward.'

'How straightforward?'

'Suicide, gunshot to the head. Ancient pistol in his left hand, big hole at his right temple, bigger one instead of the left side of his head. I recognised him straight away. Even before I bagged his warrant card. I've left bags for the gun and in case we missed anything.'

'I doubt you have.'

She looked back at the corpse: 'Shame, retiring soon, wasn't he?'

'Yeah...Ok, thanks Jean. And I am sorry.'

'It's not me you need to apologise to, is it?'

The SOCO and sidekick left, dropping a plastic wrapped packet of overshoes at our feet.

McCrackers' head was a mess. But in spite of it, he looked as composed as he ever had in life.

'Not so straightforward as all that, Grant.' I toed the gun out of McCrackers' hand.

'Why? Not left-handed?'

'No... look at the gun.'

'Old... Obviously still works. Revolver. What's it called again?'

'It's called a Webley. McCrackers' told me a story about his father's Webley once. The Webley – and how his dad died.'

'So quite straightforward: like father, like son, eh?'

'No. No, it's not. He gave his father's gun to me. It's in the boot of your car.'

'Maybe he got another one.'

'Do you really think so? Anyway, there's the other thing.'

'What?'

'Just do what I do, exactly!'

I made a pistol with my left-hand fingers. Grant did the same. We put the guns to our right temple.

'Now close your right eye: can you see the gun?'

'No, but I can feel the barrel, I won't miss.'

'But you can't see it can you?'

'No, but so what?'

'McCrackers was blind in that eye: he wouldn't have done it like that. He wouldn't. Even if he did it – he'd have swallowed the barrel. I bet that's what his dad did.'

Grant shivered: 'I expect we could find out.'

'Well, we'll do the next of kin. And I am going to ask, for sure.'

We bagged the gun. I took a last look at McCrackers. The station would be less lively now. We let Fatty in to do his worst, which was no doubt what it would be. There must have been an awful lot of bodies 'pronounced-dead-at-the-scene' hours after the event over the last few years.

Back at the station, I sent Grant to personnel to find the NOK, while I had a last look around McCrackers office. It was locked. Such a shame to break something so new as that lock, but there we were. As it went, it was pointless. The name on the door hadn't been changed, but everything else had. Better furniture, personal touches, vanity wall: the very anonymity of McCrackers' office had marked it out as different, I realised. Except for the faces in the family photographs on the desk, it was identical to any senior officer's sanctum, now. There was nothing for me there.

Grant was leaning against the reception desk. She waved a sheet of paper at me:

'Got it. You won't like it.'

'Why not?' She showed me the paper.

'Eastbourne? Fucking Eastbourne? Who lives in Eastbourne?'

'McCrackers' sister apparently.'

'Is there a phone number?'

Grant's jaw dropped. "You're not..?'

'No of course not. I'm going to phone and make sure we don't waste a whole day.'

It was a lie. I *had* been going to tell her her brother was dead over the phone.

Chapter 21

On The Wallpaper

I slept the whole of the drive down. Carmel McCracken lived in a basement flat, too many streets back from the sea-front. There was chintz at the window. A bird-like woman of about sixty-five let us in and I was glad not to have to give her the news on the doorstep. 'Have some bad news' had been password enough. She offered us tea. I declined:

'Ye'll have some fockin' Tea with me!' I tried not to smile.

'Of course, Miss McCracken, let me make it.' Grant offered.

The tiny woman managed to give Grant a look that seemed to come from a superior height:

'I'll not be letting some English proddy bitch in my fockin' kitchen.'

The china was as bone delicate as the woman's tiny fingers, and the biscuits were home made. I wondered who ate them, in normal circumstances.

She sat in a high-backed chair, looked at the proddy bitch, then turned to me; 'So, how did the big bollox die? Heart attack?'

'I'm afraid not, Miss. It appears to be suicide.'

The beautiful china smashed on the floor as she leapt to her feet; her finger pointed dangerously close to my eye: 'Shite, shite, shite. Mr Policeman. Never. Not on yer miserable proddy life.'

Grant tried to calm her down: 'Miss McCracken it's only natural...'

'Fuck. Off. You. English. Cow!'

She turned back to me:

'I found Dad you know. I had to tell Doug. I gave him the gun, afterwards, when I got the Polis to give it back.' She stopped.

'It was the gun, wasn't it? The Webley?'

'It was a Webley. Not the Webley, I've got that.'

'He gave it to you? Well you know then!'

'Miss McCracken, I appreciate it's difficult-'

'Spit it out, you Scottish wimp!'

'How did... I mean your father?' I couldn't get it out.

'The barrel was in his mouth and the back of his skull was on the wallpaper.'

'Thank you, Miss McCracken. No matter what you hear, your brother wasn't a coward, I promise you that. We'll let ourselves out.'

We did. I saw her shoulders shaking through the chintz bordered window. I guessed it wasn't anger.

Leaving Eastbourne, what sun we'd had that day was sinking fast. I looked at Grant, she seemed unbothered by the curfew: 'Hey, we're not going to make London by nightfall. No-one's done it in less than two hours in years.'

'What about a Hotel?' She glanced over at me.

'We're off the map, I don't want to check in with papers, ID deposit in the safe, all that shit. I haven't got the Euros for a deal that dirty.'

'I have.'

'They'll name their price after dark. You'll need more cash than a Saudi arms deal.'

'I said I'd cover it.'

Where she had the money I didn't know; unless there was a false bottom in her suitcase. If there was, she'd taken a few too many chances that day.

'Brighton then.' I gave in.

'I know Brighton, someone I knew used to live there.'

'Did they? How very nice for them.'

'You can pay next time.' She said.

It was almost dusk as the Mini pulled up in Oriental Place, outside a hotel that a web-site might once have described as funky. Nothing fades as fast as fashion. Grant opened the boot. I took out the gun, she took out the case. We went up the steps into the Hotel. A guy about my age was behind the desk sporting an improbable tan. He looked out the window at the darkening sky. Shook his head. Grant opened the case, slapped a wad of notes on the desk in front of him. The guy shrugged; I saw a line of white emerge from his collar where the spray-on stopped. He pushed a book towards us;

'Put check in time as four pm, ID cards... Please.'

The manners were an afterthought. After he saw my face.

'Count the money. We're not here - all night - alright.' Grant said.

He seemed about to argue, thought better of it, handed us a key. I looked at his fingers on the ludicrously sized fob.

'Where's the smoke room?' I leaned over the desk at him.

'Don't be daft.'

'Don't you be; don't tell me you don't smoke all shift. Where is it?'

'I'll show you.'

I told Grant I'd see her upstairs in room 101, flipped her the key, which she caught without appearing to move her hand in the slightest.

The smoke room was in the basement. The laundry room in fact. Ideal: the huge extractor was drawing out the smoke the five of us were churning out. No one spoke. Just wary-eyed nods in greeting. It used to be more social; smoking. In this kind of place it became the furtive, criminalised act homosexuality had been before I was born. I preferred the Number Six and places like it. But then, I was a policeman, easier for me - and for real criminals - not to care. Joe Soap had no such choices. The others drifted out through the door like the smoke towards the fan. I settled down for the night: guaranteeing at least one of us a decent night's sleep.

The door was barged open at 7 am. It was the Tanfaker: come for his last fag before going home.

'Fuck, you must be an addict.' He started when he saw me.

'A desperate man.' I replied.

'Breakfast's on in the dining room; the staff know you're "specials." Order what you want.'

Everything had its price; even a full English. Or Kippers? My mouth watered, but I knew I'd be ordering a drink instead.

Grant arrived at 7.30. Sat opposite. Said nothing. A waitress arrived, took the menu from Grant's hand:

'For special customers we have Full English, Full American, Kippers, Devilled Kidneys and your choice of tea or coffee with pasteurised milk.'

Grant looked at my glass.

'What about orange juice?'

The waitress smirked: 'Would that be with or without champagne?'

I shrugged.

Grant snapped at the waitress : 'Never mind. Tea with milk. American Breakfast, no pancakes.'

The waitress scribbled something hieroglyphic on her pad. Since we were near the kitchen we both heard her yell 'Full English' on the other side of the door. I laughed. Grant almost cracked a smile.

She bit her lip. 'It's not proof you know.'

'What, the gun?'

'Of course, the gun!'

'Well it is you know, in a way.'

'Don't be ridiculous.' No 'guv'.

'Why do you think he gave it to me?'

'I don't know. You needed it more than him? So he wouldn't use it on himself?'

'No, it was a kind of message.'

'Come on.' She sneered.

Her breakfast arrived. She set about it. Demolished it. Wiped a stray rivulet of yellow from the corner of her mouth with a finger and sucked the yoke greedily from it.

'How is it a message?' she said.

'He couldn't have used it on himself actually. It's decommissioned.'

'Eh?'

'Oh, it looks OK, but there's no firing pin.'

'He gave you a useless gun?'

'No, I think it's very useful. Very useful indeed.'

We made our appearance in CID at 11, around 3 hours: good time; bad timing. Elvis had appeared too, most of the task force in tow. Fritz had new battle scars by the look of it, Off-Cut, on his coat-tails as usual, had a few of his own. And George Hewson was there. No uniform, I gave him a jerky nod. He'd chosen his side then. Ari seemed on the periphery of it all: my former partner gave me an even shorter nod. They were all smiles and camaraderie; Joyous, Elvis's driver would be outside in the car. The jokes would be off-colour in every sense. The group had the end-of-term look policemen in the pub used to have when they'd cracked a big case. I motioned Grant towards my desk,

'Guess which side's yours.' I said.

'My side's the messy side.'

'I meant the desk.'

'I didn't.' She smiled.

I started writing a report. Grant looked around bored, until one of the TVs caught her eye. I turned to look at it. Elvis and pals were looking up at the screen. Kilgour was in a studio. On a sofa, a soft interview then. The interviewer was the Token. Grant shouted:

'Turn it up.' Fritz waved the remote at the screen. I looked at the Token's legs.

Kilgour's voice melted into the room: 'Of course we all hope Jackie can return to Parliament in the fullness of time, the strain of recent events has taken its toll. I can assure you she is in the best of hands and we all wish her a speedy recovery.'

The Token got full-beam from Kilgour and all of a sudden she was leaning forward and her legs were crossed just like Uncle Mac's apart from the killer-heeled shoe dangling from her toes. I rolled my eyes at Grant, but she didn't notice. There were shouts of 'Yesss!' and 'Result!'

from the Elvis fan club.

On his way out, Elvis leaned over Grant's shoulder:

'That your report on the Kilburn body?'

'Yes.'

His mouth went thin: 'Suicide, hmm! Always a candidate, really though, what with his father and all, eh?'

'Some candidates you just can't bring yourself to vote for, sir.'

'Sometimes the choice shouldn't be left to the people.'

Much as I liked seeing the back of him, that erect posture was beginning to get to me. I needed to let off steam, Grant was still miles away. Fritz was holding court over the gang now.

'Hey Fritz, how many kids did you beat up last night?'

'Fuck off, Murray. It's our business, what we did.'

He was standing next to Off-Cut, who was nodding his pointy head at about Fritz's chest level. Little and large. And it struck me that it wasn't just their business, it was mine too.

'Come on, Grant. I need a shower. You can drive me home. Northwood.'

'Northwood? Shit, that'll take ages.'

'Got a date?'

'No, but...'

'Welcome to CID.'

It was almost dusk as the Mini pulled up in Oriental Place, outside a hotel that a web-site might once have described as funky. Nothing fades as fast as fashion. Grant opened the boot. I took out the gun, she took out the case. We went up the steps into the Hotel. A guy about my age was behind the desk sporting an improbable tan. He looked out the window at the darkening sky. Shook his head. Grant opened the case, slapped a wad of notes on the desk in front of him. The guy shrugged; I saw a line of white emerge from his collar where the spray-on stopped. He pushed a book towards us;

'Put check in time as four pm, ID cards... Please.'

The manners were an afterthought. After he saw my face.

'Count the money. We're not here - all night - alright.' Grant said.

He seemed about to argue, thought better of it, handed us a key. I looked at his fingers on the ludicrously sized fob.

'Where's the smoke room?' I leaned over the desk at him.

'Don't be daft.'

'Don't you be; don't tell me you don't smoke all shift. Where is it?'

'I'll show you.'

I told Grant I'd see her upstairs in room 101, flipped her the key, which she caught without appearing to move her hand in the slightest.

The smoke room was in the basement. The laundry room in fact. Ideal: the huge extractor was drawing out the smoke the five of us were churning out. No one spoke. Just wary-eyed nods in greeting. It used to be more social; smoking. In this kind of place it became the furtive, criminalised act homosexuality had been before I was born. I preferred the Number Six and places like it. But then, I was a policeman, easier for me - and for real criminals - not to care. Joe Soap had no such choices. The others drifted out through the door like the smoke towards the fan. I settled down for the night: guaranteeing at least one of us a decent night's sleep.

The door was barged open at 7 am. It was the Tanfaker: come for his last fag before going home.

'Fuck, you must be an addict.' He started when he saw me.

'A desperate man.' I replied.

'Breakfast's on in the dining room; the staff know you're "specials." Order what you want.'

Everything had its price; even a full English. Or Kippers? My mouth watered, but I knew I'd be ordering a drink instead.

Grant arrived at 7.30. Sat opposite. Said nothing. A waitress arrived, took the menu from Grant's hand: 'For special customers we have Full English, Full American, Kippers, Devilled Kidneys and your choice of tea or coffee with pasteurised milk.'

Grant looked at my glass. 'What about orange juice?'

The waitress smirked: 'Would that be with or without champagne?'

I shrugged.

Grant snapped at the waitress : 'Never mind. Tea with milk. American Breakfast, no pancakes.'

The waitress scribbled something hieroglyphic on her pad. Since we were near the kitchen we both heard her yell 'Full English' on the other side of the door. I laughed. Grant almost cracked a smile.

She bit her lip. 'It's not proof you know.'

'What the gun?'

'Of course, the gun!'

'Well it is you know, in a way.'

'Don't be ridiculous.' No 'guv'.

'Why do you think he gave it to me?'

'I don't know. You needed it more than him? So he wouldn't use it on himself?'

'No, it was a kind of message.'

'Come on.' She sneered.

Her breakfast arrived. She set about it. Demolished it. Wiped a stray rivulet of yellow from the corner of her mouth with a finger and sucked the yoke greedily from it.

'How is it a message?' she said.

'He couldn't have used it on himself actually. It's decommissioned.'

'Eh?'

'Oh, it looks OK, but there's no firing pin.'

'He gave you a useless gun?'

'No, I think it's very useful. Very useful indeed.'

We made our appearance in CID at 11, around 3 hours: good time; bad timing. Elvis had appeared too, most of the task force in tow. Fritz had new battle scars by the look of it, Off-Cut, on his coat-tails as usual, had a few of his own. And George Hewson was there. No uniform, I gave him a jerky nod. He'd chosen his side then. Ari seemed on the periphery of it all: my former partner gave me an even shorter nod. They were all smiles and camaraderie; Joyous, Elvis's driver would be outside in the car. The jokes would be off-colour in every sense. The group had the end-of-term look policemen in the pub used to have when they'd cracked a big case. I motioned Grant towards my desk, 'Guess which side's yours.' I said.

'My side's the messy side.'

'I meant the desk.'

'I didn't.' She smiled.

I started writing a report. Grant looked around bored, until one of the TVs caught her eye. I turned to look at it. Elvis and pals were looking up at the screen. Kilgour was in a studio. On a sofa, a soft interview then. The interviewer was the Token. Grant shouted:

'Turn it up.'

Fritz waved the remote at the screen. I looked at the Token's legs.

Kilgour's voice melted into the room:

'Of course we all hope Jackie can return to Parliament in the fullness of time, the strain of recent events has taken its toll. I can assure you she is in the best of hands and we all wish her a speedy recovery.'

The Token got full-beam from Kilgour and all of a sudden she was leaning forward and her legs were crossed just like Uncle Mac's apart from the killer-heeled shoe dangling from her toes. I rolled my eyes at Grant, but she didn't notice. There were shouts of 'Yess!' and 'Result!' from the Elvis fan club.

On his way out, Elvis leaned over Grant's shoulder,

'That your report on the Kilburn body?'

'Yes.'

His mouth went thin: 'Suicide, hmm! Always a candidate, really though, what with his father and all, eh?'

'Some candidates you just can't bring yourself to vote for, sir.' I said.

'Sometimes the choice shouldn't be left to the people.'

Much as I liked seeing the back of him, that erect posture was beginning to get to me. I needed to let off steam, Grant was still miles away. Fritz was holding court over the gang now.

'Hey Fritz, how many kids did you beat up last night?'

'Fuck off, Murray. It's our business, what we did.'

He was standing next to Off-Cut, who was nodding his pointy head at about Fritz's chest level. Little and large. And it struck me that it wasn't just their business, it was mine too.

'Come on, Grant. I need a shower. You can drive me home. Northwood,'

'Northwood? Shit, that'll take ages.'

'Got a date?'

'No, but...'

'Welcome to CID.'

Chapter 22

"Coffee, tea or me?"

On the drive out, we passed tanks, APCs, canvas-sided three-tonners full of troops. Whether they were going to an operation or returning from one, I couldn't tell. It meant something though. The Armed Forces hadn't quite reached the cabbage-stealing nadir of the Russians in the 90's, but the Defence Budget hadn't even run to paper manoeuvres for the last few years. Yes, the odd Civil Disobedience intervention like those of the last few nights. But this? Not a chance.

In front of the semi in Kewsferry Road, I said to Grant:

'Come in if you want. I'm going to get some stuff, have a shower.'

She grunted but followed me to the front door. I used my Yale. Inside the hallway wasn't too bad. The telephone was in pieces on the floor, next to the pieces of the table it used to sit on. The pictures were still on the walls, skewiff, Picasso-fied by the crazing on the glass in the frames.

I went into the lounge. I stood amongst the plastic, paper and silver discs. Grant bent down, picked up a disc, looked at both sides:

'I didn't know anyone still had these. They take up so much room'

'You should have seen vinyl.' I said.

'Burglary?'

'I don't think so.' I pointed at the smashed screen of the TV.

I walked through the rest of the ground floor. Every drawer's contents were on the floor. At the bedroom door I turned and held up a hand:

'Wait here.' I had a quick look inside. Started to head back down.

'Don't you want to...' She started.

'No, I don't. And neither do you.'

We went to the kitchen. I found two cups, no handles but intact, put the kettle on.

'Coffee, tea or me?'

'Ask me again after your shower, coffee. Black.'

We watched the kettle boil for a while.

'What was that about upstairs?'

'It isn't a burglary, nothing's gone. They left something though. The burglar's calling card.'

'You mean...'

'Call it another message. You make the brews. I'll go back up and see if there are any clothes left I can wear.'

The smell was bad. I found some wearable stuff on the floor. It would be the unstructured look for a few days. Then I wrapped the DNA-filled evidence and the clothes underneath it in the quilt they were both on lying on. The bundle went to the bin out front. I came back for my brew.

'I reckon I'll put this place on the market.'

'Over this?'

'No, I just don't need it any more.' I said.

My damp hair was drying against the headrest. We'd stopped off in the town centre. The estate agent had been a dinner party guest whenI was still presentable enough to meet members of Yol's social network. Didn't remember me, of course, but damn few forgot Yol. I never would, in spite of everything. Yol had given our son a name. I never used it: not once in seven days and not in the five years since. Vicky had never even seen her younger brother. I had to admit; he was an 'elastoplast baby': to repair the wounds in our marriage. But he died, and the wounds became gangrenous - and I should have been amputated long ago.

'Penny for them,' Grant said.

'Rather have a euro.'

'Jeez, inflation or what.'

'Well I could have said cent; but you've probably never seen one.'

'Have though.' She hesitated.

'Yeah, I should have known... one of Uncle Mac's Junkets, eh?'

'It was a long time ago. I was still at Uni.'

'Jesus, Uni. I bet you're popular with the older plod.'

'What?'

'When I joined; we used to take the piss out of the Fast Track Graduates. Most of them stopped mentioning degrees, education or "Uni" within the first week.'

'Yeah, well. No need now is there.'

'Made CID without Fast Track though, didn't you?'

'Not without sharp practice.'

We arrived at CID in the nick. In the nick of time, in fact. Fritz and Off-Cut were at our desk: the contents were on the floor. Off-Cut sidled round behind Fritz. Fritz held an old Police Gazette between finger and thumb.

'Might be valuable this, hey? To a collector?'

'Could be, Fritz. Did you think it was porn?'

He dropped the magazine in curiously effete gesture, like a 19th century heroine dropping a 'kerchief.

'Well. Just been doing a bit of sorting out for you, Murray. You got anything we need in here, or can we give up?'

'Nope; no porn, no Combat 13, no Soldier of Fortune – not even a Beano.'

'You'll get yours, Murray – and I'll be giving it to you.'

'Yeah, we will,' said Off-Cut.

They left. I looked at the damage. There really was nothing to find. It seemed that the former Task Force spent more time in my nick than I did. But then, I'd transferred a new DC in off my own bat, completely unmarked by the batting of eyelids. We cleared up. I threw out all sorts of junk; even the Police Gazette. Grant fished it out of the wastepaper:

'Looks familiar.' She pointed at a fresh-faced PC on the cover. He was proudly holding a velvet-lined box for the camera.

'I used to know him too.'

'What did he get? What is it? OBE, MBE?'

'It was the George Medal.'

I took the magazine and tossed it back in the wastepaper basket. The tarnished medal was with the befouled clothes, wrapped in a quilt in a Northwood skip.

CID was deserted now except for us. Grant was making a desultory tour of the other 7 desks. She held up a Standard.

'Late edition. Front page might interest you.'

'I doubt it.'

'Uncle Mac's in charge. The King apparently asked him to form a government. Requested that Emergency Powers be invoked.'

'Sure he did. Probably thought he was talking to a begonia.'

'Well, anyway. You should take a look.'

The headline wasn't massive. It was a quote.

'We need strong leadership.'

I wondered what a begonia would have answered to that. Reading the article, I found it short on detail, long on conjecture. It wasn't Needles' best work. I turned to the inside pages. McCrackers got a 4 inch column: unnamed Police sources said the evidence pointed towards suicide. Good strategy, get your version in the Public Domain first. It's usually the one that sticks, whatever comes later. Grant appeared at my shoulder:

'Page 3, the bottom right. Tiny print.'

" Former Foreign Secretary admitted to Priory " headed about 3 lines with the sketchiest of personal details.

'Won't see her again in a hurry.' I said.

'People do get out of those places you know.'

'They used to when it was a Celeb rehab unit.'

'I'm sure it's the best place for her.'

'A few other people think so too, evidently.'

What boat couldn't they risk her rocking? Was she the kind of politician prepared to damage her own reputation by doing so? Or was she really suffering form 'nervous exhaustion?' I doubted I'd ever find out.

My mobile beeped. Beeped again. 2 SMSs:

'18.00 Been @ #6 since 4. Where you? Needles.'

'20.00 Meeting McCrackers in Soho. Call me 2mrw. Needles.'

'Fuck! Almost 24 hours for a message to come through. Take a look.'

I handed her the phone.

'Fuck is right. Wonder who Needles was going to rap the table with.'

'Eh?'

'Guv, sometimes you are slow. McCrackers? Yesterday? He was already dead.'

I lifted the landline on the nearest desk.

'Read out Needles number, Grant.'

Take one of the mobiles out of the equation and I might get through.

'Shit! Unobtainable. Text him. At the Six, as soon as. I think we'll put all our eggs in Woodbine's basket. I'm going to give him the cassette-tape too.'

'

Chapter 23

"Remind me, D'Artagnan"

The door of the Number Six was locked. The hands on my watch told me that couldn't be true. It was 4 in the afternoon. I smashed the filthy window next to the locked door.

'Smell it?' I said.

'Smoke?' She sniggered.

'Yeah, not tobacco.'

I wrapped my jacket round my arm, knocked out as much glass as I could. Tried to get through the window. Too fat, too old. Grant shoved me out of the way. Glad she'd worn trousers today. Me too. I shoved the jacket in after her:

'For the smoke.'

It was a long two minutes. The door opened, Grant and Woodbine fell out, coughing. Insulating tape dangled from one cheek on Woodbine's face.

'Get moving, there's butane on the premises.' He said.

We hunkered down behind Grant's car. Woodbine was still coughing, the warning must have taken some effort. Grant was just about OK. Her eyes were still watering, she looked very white. I slapped her face.

'Hey!! What was that for?'

'Shock.' I said.

'It was.'

'Inside, what did you see?'

'Smoke.'

'Come on.'

There was a massive bang. The front wall of the building appeared to bulge for a second and then burst. The car took a few hits, but most of the rubble sailed over our heads. The shock wave didn't. The Mini rocked and I thought we'd end up under it. Grant's mouth was moving; I couldn't hear anything. My mouth moved. I still couldn't hear anything. The three of us sat on the pavement, leaned our backs against the side of the car. I lit a cigarette. Offered one to Woodbine. He looked like he was coughing. All I could hear was buzzing. The glass in the Mini's windows was crazed. I hoped the car would still go.

The façade of the building opposite the Number Six showed how lucky we'd been. The blast had blown the windows in: there was a beer barrel at the front door; it had cleared the car and somersaulted to stand upright on the step. It stood sentinel for the solicitor's, accountants' and Insurance Brokers' offices housed in the building.

I could hear a faint voice under the buzzing: Grant. Her face was stretching and contracting violently around her mouth. She must have been shouting: 'Et et ooving.'

I shrugged. She put her lips to my ear. Her exaggerated mouth movements denied the moment any erotic thrill.

'Let's get moving.'

Grant swung the driver door wide and hard. Elbowed the glass from inside to out. She sat in the driver's seat and started punching the windscreen outwards. I helped her. Pointing at Woodbine, she mimed getting him into the back. It would be tight squeeze. He seemed out of it. I got him in from the passenger side, eventually. I shut the passenger door gingerly. Bashed out the rest of the glass with an elbow. She floored the pedal and the engine noise was welcome. I wondered how loud it really was.

I tapped Grant's arm : 'Where are we GOING?'

She shook her head. Shrugged. Conversation too difficult.

Eventually she pulled up at a railway arch MOT Centre; a skinhead in pristine overalls was pulling down the security shutter. He did a double take: said something. I still couldn't make it out. A very clean-fingernailed hand shook Grant's. He walked round the car, shaking his head. Woodbine was alert. We got out of the car. I sat on a low wall nearby, wondering if my hearing would come back. There was an animated conversation between Grant and Mr Clean. The shutter went back up. Woodbine was still standing, mumbling to himself. Mr Clean drove the Mini in. A few minutes later he drove a tatty Focus out, handed Grant the keys. Grant motioned us into the car. A four-door this time. A shove on Woodbine's well padded arse got him in the back. I heard the slam of the door as Grant got in: 'Who the fuck was that?'

'Stop shouting!' she whispered.

'Well who?' I 'whispered' back.

'My brother.' And either the Focus's engine was louder, or my hearing was coming back.

We pulled up in Soho, not far from Berwick Street. A paper shop and convenience store on the corner. The Focus had two wheels on the pavement so the car was straddling the faded yellow lines. Further up the street, jagged mouthed poles marked where the yellow lines stopped and the meters used to stand. The shop was open. It was the kind of shop the South Asians used to run. A large, white male with the shaved look favoured by the male-pattern balding was behind the counter. Grant waved a bunch of keys at him.

'Mac gave me the keys.'

The guy nodded but eyed me and Woodbine with suspicion as we trooped behind Grant to the stairs at the back. At the top of the stairs Grant let us into a flat. The corner building must have measured a great many square feet.

'Mac?' I said.

'Mac. He's Macaulay too.'

'What are we doing here?'

'I need to tell you some stuff.'

I pointed at Woodbine. 'Why's he here?'

'So does he.'

The flat was open plan: lucite worktops, clean-lined doors in the kitchen. Sharp, straight lines everywhere. Too much white for a family. Too much money for a mechanic, or even the owner of a garage. My hearing was back. With something extra, the buzzing was a ringing now. Like a distant burglar alarm in the background.

'Nice place,' I said.

'You want a coffee?' Grant asked.

'Yeah.'

'Woodbine?'

He shook his head. He looked like some arty composition, so dark against the sofa. The coffee was black and very sweet. Grant gave Woodbine some sweet and sticky gloop from the American-style fridge. Sugar for shock.

'So,' I said. 'Tell me.'

'You think you know about me and Uncle Mac?'

'I didn't say that.'

'You didn't have to.'

She sat on a tubular steel and white leather chair. I pulled out something angular and uncomfortable from the dining table.

'We knew him from Christmas cards, Birthday cards and, occasionally, newspapers. The financials. Mummy read them out. Every article started "Falklands War hero..." That was the only bit we could understand then. He came for the first time, in 95. I was 10 I think, my brother was 12, back from school at the end of the First Year. We lived in Harrogate.'

Grant pronounced this Harrow-gate and it was obvious what kind of house they'd lived in.

'Over 20 years ago, he still looked pretty much the same. The week before he arrived Mummy cleaned before and after the daily came. He brought presents. Right from the very beginning.'

She fingered a three-coloured-gold bracelet on her wrist; it looked a little snug. I thought it was a grown-up present to give a 10-year old.

'That first time, a man in the house. At night. Daddy was a photograph. A uniformed man in a photograph. Just that one picture. When he arrived, we had tea. Scones. "Pleased to meet you, sir."
My brother shook his hand.

"Call me Uncle Mac." My brother said, "My name's Mac, too.'

Grant took a sip of her coffee, didn't even make a face. My mug was empty, her drink must have been freezing.

'After tea, he showed my brother and I other photographs. The three of them: my mum, him and my father looking like students. Then it was he and my father in uniforms. Smart ones, ceremonial ones, ones for dying in. We knew Daddy had died in the Falklands of course. Uncle Mac told us a story about how it happened. Said Daddy should have got the Medal, not him. Anyway, Uncle Mac said he thought he should look after us, it was what his friend would have wanted. And Mummy started crying.'

She licked her lips, shifted in the leather chair as though it were as uncomfortable as the one I sat in.

'I slept on put-you-up in my brother's bedroom, that night. Uncle Mac said he was glad he would have my bed. He started coming at birthdays, Christmas. If he was on business in the North.'

She stopped, if she'd been a smoker, she'd have lit up. No-one smoked in private accommodation, anyway. Smoke alarms were linked to security alarms on the outside of buildings. It was more efficient than the informers. Smoke-easys paid firemen, policemen and health and safety inspectors off. Private citizens couldn't afford to.

'It was my 12th birthday. Little Mac would have been 14. Midnight. We were awake, he was being gross as only teenage boys can, I was sensitive, hormonal, if you like. I whisper-shouted at him: "I'm telling Uncle Mac, right now."

'I burst into my bedroom. Of course, the bed was empty.'

Grant looked me in the eye. Waiting for me to say something. I had nothing to say. Woodbine was asleep, the dregs of the gloop staining the white of the sofa a livid puce.

'I didn't see Uncle Mac again, until I went to Uni. I thought that was my fault, of course. He was making his bid for political power in Scotland, so it was back to cards and newspapers. My first day at St Andrews, he met me with flowers and money. I was flattered; an important figure in the Scottish Parliament coming to see me.

'Actually he was making a speech about closing down the Air Force base nearby.' She let out a long sigh: 'But it's all about you, when you're 18 years old.'

She stopped.

'I wish I could remember.' I said.

'I slept with him, off and on, throughout University.'

For a moment, I thought she wasn't aware of what she'd done. But I looked at her face, it had gone hard, and I could see what she'd look like in 15 years or so.

'The car wasn't a graduation present. He bought it for me, afterwards. After the clinic. He's paid for the maintenance on it ever since.'

She stopped again. And this time I knew I wasn't expected to say anything.

Woodbine jerked awake. How much he'd heard or how much he already knew, I didn't know. The very last drops of the gloop landed on his trousers: a very plummy 'Fuck!' rang out. He looked from me to Grant.

'Everyone has to live down to their image, don't they?'

'Feeling better?'

'Headache, noise in my ears.'

'I've had worse hangovers, though.'

'Me too.'

Grant spoke; monotone with a tremble, like a McCrackers outburst if they'd given him lithium.

'Tell him. Tell him what you told me, the other day, before he woke up.'

Woodbine leaned back into the sofa, looked into the distance, into another life.

'I went to school with Grant's brother. In the same year; not friends. I didn't have many. Just the Arabs or the Jews, these places liked their money, if only they hadn't had to put up with their offspring. My dad's money had me in the school, too. My dad was rich; I don't know where the money came from, not even now. He brought it with him from Jamaica. It paid for a degree of respectability, acceptance and my education. It's not important.'

He looked down at the stain on the sofa, brushed it absently. No hope of wiping it away.

'He was called Grant Minor at school. There was another older Grant; didn't matter they weren't related. He was younger; he was Minor. We were in the fourth form; a year to go before GCSEs. I'd gone behind the cricket pavilion to smoke. Everyone else was watching the match. I'd just been run out by a chinless prick who thought it was his God-given right to score off every ball.'

Woodbine looked about to spit, but thought better of it.

'Grant was blubbing. Bad form, in public, in public school. I was uncomfortable. "Come on, old chap." Yeah, I talked like that. It's important to fit in. He just kept blubbing. "What's up?" I said, although I didn't really care. He said his Uncle was coming, to take him away for the Exeat. "I wish someone would take me out at the weekends." I said. He said I didn't understand. That his Uncle was like FForbes and Crosby in the VIth. I asked him how long it had been going on. He said since he was 12. What was there to say? I felt sorry for him. Spoke to him about 5 times after that. He left after his GCSEs.'

The chemical zombie voice spoke again:

'My brother joined the Army at 16, following in Daddy's footsteps.'

Both of them, I thought.

'I knew something was up, of course. He wouldn't talk about it, never did. I told him I knew, tonight, at the Arches. He'll be here soon.'

It was difficult to decide what it all meant, if anything. It surely had little to do with Smokescreen. Kilgour's immorality had little to do with fitness for public life, did it? Not if history was anything to go by. I was suddenly sick of it, sick of it all. My wife and daughter had done the right thing, after all – as long as they made it.

The door burst open. Little Mac took all three in at a glance. Peered at Woodbine a little longer than at me. Then he shook his head walked over to his sister. There was an awkward embrace; they shared the same good looks. Shared genes.

Woodbine stood up, hand extended.

'Charlton Woodbine.'

Little Mac shook the hand warily. 'Macaulay, Macaulay Grant. You were at the school.'

Woodbine nodded: 'Yeah, well. It was a long time ago.'

'I suppose.' Said Little Mac, I didn't think it was for him.

'The Smart Disk's gone, is it?.' I asked Woodbine.

He grinned. It still jarred, seeing the stone face moving. He rooted about in a trouser pocket, the gloop stain moving as he fumbled. Then he showed me 3 SD cards in the palm of one hand.

'I don't suppose it matters anyway. Jackie Carlton's chewing carpets at the Priory.'

'Don't be too sure,' he said. He looked at Little Mac: 'got a laptop?'

He nodded and picked up a slim metallic looking thing that looked as expensive as a new car. He saw me looking.

'You know, I take it?' Woodbine and I nodded. 'I blackmail him.' He said matter of factly.

'D'you mind?'

Woodbine opened the laptop on the dining table, powered it up, inserted one of the cards:

'I've got a confession to make, my sister's my 'Geekster.' She works at Barclays de Zoute. Most guys in the know use the banking system for any computer work. You can hide anything in their systems... They do, after all.'

We obliged him with a laugh.

'Anyway, she told me the data had been edited.'

He looked from Grant, to me, to Grant's brother:

'You know this stuff normally has a date/time stamp in one corner, right? Worthless as evidence otherwise, right?'

'So?' I said.

'Well, look. This is your original. No time, date nothing.'

He removed the Smart Disk. Replaced it with another:

There in the corner, was the date:

'Is it evidence though?'

'Yep, the first card has the information on it. You can't really get rid of anything, stuff on computer media is like a cockroach, it'll survive nuclear winter. Once you write something, it can always be read. By someone.'

The date in the corner was two days before the PM had died.

Woodbine shut down the lap-top. I felt tired, I went over to the fridge and pulled out one of those pathetically-sized designer beers, Sol or something: had a twist cap anyway. I raised the bottle to Little Mac: 'Here's to blackmail, crime pays well if you can afford this.'

'You might offer them round, if you feel so at home.' He said.

But he got a bottle out for himself and Woodbine. Nothing for little sis. Little Mac noticed the silence was awkward, picked up a remote and aimed it over his shoulder like an Annie Oakley trick-shot. The plasma lit up immediately. Great picture, but the programming was dire.

'Shit!' This was Woodbine; we all turned to look at the screen.

The Number Six was in the background, blackened by smoke and wrecked by the blast. The upper two floors had collapsed into the basement like a cake when someone opened the oven door too soon. Flabby Flak Jacket had his microphone shoved in another familiar face:

'...It looks very much as though the unlicensed bar in the building's basement was being used as an illegal smoking den...'

As Ari Chryssipous had been smoking in it within the last few days, he knew whereof he spoke.

'...we're very anxious to contact this man...' He went on. A truly awful mug shot of Woodbine flashed up, 10 years out of date, with the waxwork expression that makes witnesses guess when confronted with pages of them.

'Mr Charlton Woodbine, aged 35. We have reason to believe he is the owner/operator of this particular smoke-easy.'

'Cunt!' Woodbine said.

I could see his point.

Ari was still speaking: 'Arson is suspected but not confirmed. As there was no-one found on the premises we have not ruled out an insurance swindle.'

'I wished I'd fucking stayed.' Woodbine shouted at the TV.

'Hey, we saw the fireworks. Why stay for the clearing up?' I said.

And we'd have been cleared up too, I saw that now.

Grant spoke, for the first time in what seemed like ages: 'What about Needles?'

'What about him? He wasn't inside was he?'

'Just me.' Said Woodbine.

'Better text him,' Grant said. 'We need to figure out how McCrackers contacted him from the other side.'

Shit, I hoped she wasn't as flaky as that made her sound.

'You mean who contacted him from the other side.' I corrected her.

The sport was just finishing up with a story on England's Euro 16 Qualifier against Slovenia. The Slovenes were complaining to UEFA that they felt London was an unsafe venue and were asking for a neutral ground as a safer location. Their manager had suggested Kosovo or Chechnya. The summary of headlines was next as usual. The Token appeared to have recovered from her encounter with Uncle Mac on the sofa and she had reverted to glossy, hard type:

'Unrest around the Soho Westminster area continued last night with a nail bomb attack on a pub in Old Compton Street; fleeing patrons were beaten with batons and chased from the vicinity by groups numbering in the hundreds. An eye witness described the groups as consisting entirely of white males. The Mayor of London, former Policeman Hugh Paddick, has asked how, with so many soldiers deployed, they are mysteriously absent from any scene of disturbance. The Home Office has declined to answer.'

'That's something,' Little Mac said.

'What?' Woodbine sighed.

'At least you weren't the top item.' He said.

'Listen, there's something else...' I pointed at the screen.

'... the Leader Macaulay Kilgour suspended the constitution today in a speech before a packed house...'

'The Leader? What's that shit?'

Woodbine ssh-sh-ed me. Grant and her brother had that look again and I knew 'The Leader' was on screen.

' Regrettably, I have had to suspend the constitution, until further notice: the civil unrest and the parlous state of services, the economy and law-and-order require a strong and virile response...'

'Good old Laura...' I said. But no-one laughed.

The news ended with the weatherman predicting more rain, and the BBC began showing a documentary on wind farms in the Cheviot Hills. The Grants returned to Earth:

'What is it with you and that man? After everything he's..' I snapped.

Little Mac interrupted : 'I don't blackmail him to get back at him, you know.'

'OK, why then?'

'Because I can't get him back.' I mimed two fingers down my throat.

'I do hate him.' His sister said: 'But he has that... that thing.'

'Oh right, that thing. That'll do it.'

'Oh come on, you've met him, charisma, charm, magnetism – whatever you want to call it!'

'Nope, never felt a thing. But I checked my watch after he shook my hand.'

'Maybe you're just jealous.' She jeered.

'If that makes you feel better.'

Woodbine told us all to grow up. He was probably right to. I texted Needles' mobile.

'I've given him this address.' Little Mac gave a nod and a shrug at the same time.

'Can we stay here, tonight?' Again the body language.

'Got any real drinks?' I said.

He went over to the kitchen, rooted about and came over with some Highland Mist malt whiskey. Gave me a glass as an afterthought.

'What about you Charlton?' He nodded.

I poured two fingers in the glass and gave it to him.

'Don't let it evaporate. I'm very thirsty.'

And I necked a belt about the size of his measure. Grant snatched the bottle from my grasp.

'We could fall out soon.' I narrowed my eyes, but they were still watering from the whiskey.

'You can have it later, we need to discuss what we're going to do.'

'Do? About what? About your megalomaniac pseudo-uncle? About the energy crisis, about the collapse in Police morale. Or do I mean morals?'

She looked down her nose at me. I squirmed in the uncomfortable dining chair:

'You now have two suspicious deaths on your hands, an attempted murder by arson and enough material for a conspiracy theory that would melt the internet, if it ever appeared. I would have thought even you might want to 'investigate."

'We haven't a chance. 'The Leader' will see to that.' I said.

'We need to try.'

'You'll be telling me next we need an honest politician.'

'Or one with nothing to lose.'

'And just what do you hope to achieve? Do you really think anyone will care about any of it? What if 'Uncle Mac' gets the trains running? And on time? What if things improve? People won't give a shit, and you know it.'

'I will.' She said.

The doorbell rang before I could answer that. Little Mac just beat his sister to the intercom.

'Needles.' Coughed out of the speaker.

Little Mac buzzed and went down into the shop. He appeared a few minutes later bearing most of Needles' weight. He looked a mess; not too much bleeding – but plenty of blood. On his clothes.

'You really should look after yourself less.' I said. 'You don't do it very well.'

He gave a sort of laugh, or perhaps a cough. Little Mac laid him on the sofa, adding a different shade to Woodbine's spillage. He began checking Needles over, looked competent, so we left him to it.

'The blood's not mine.' Needles said.

'How did McCrackers get in touch?' I asked.

'Voice mail at the Standard.'

'Sure it was him?'

'Oh yeah?'

'When did he leave the message?'

'Yesterday, I think.'

'Don't you know?' Grant said.

'The messages are dumped onto my computer daily or at 25 messages, the phone system's old. Limited storage. No date-stamp info, saves time and space.'

'So it could have been the day before or anything?'

'Well if someone overrode the autodump, it could have been anytime.'

'You don't read your own paper, do you?'

'Not likely, I haven't read a paper since the Guardian went.'

'Maybe you should,' Grant said. 'Your paper reported his death today.'

Woodbine looked at Needles: 'So whose is it? The blood.'

'Not who, what?'

'What are you on about?' I was missing the bottle, which Grant was emptying into Needles.

'It's sheep's blood.'

'Don't give him any more,' I said.

'No, let me tell it, Murray. It won't take long.'

It didn't. He'd turned up at The Number One Club in Soho as requested: before he'd rung the bell he'd been bundled into the back of a van by two men, one tall one short. They'd worn hoods. He rattled about in the back of the van, getting the occasional slap from the hooded guys. The van stopped. His hands were tied. They took him into a large warehouse type building. He saw shapes dangling from hooks. The tall guy and his shrimp pal hooked his tied hands, they dangled him too. He smelt blood and meat. Needles described a ride on the hook as it ran on a rail to a separate part of the warehouse, There was a racket; insanely loud bleating. A lamb was winched up on a hook beside him. Then another. Then another. The tall man slit their throats and all three winched a lamb each to the top of a block and tackle. The hoods weaved in and out of the raining blood to give him a beating. He passed out. Some Moslem workers had let him out a few hours ago.

'Didn't the hoods say anything?' I asked.

'They just said I'd had a warning before, and there wouldn't be another.'

'So why are you here?' Grant peered at him.

'I've never liked doing what I'm told.'

Grant looked pleased, Woodbine nodded his respect, Little Mac's eyes looked a little glazed. I snatched the bottle from Grant, made my eyes water again. Put the bottle on the dining table. I looked round at the four tautly tired faces, Grant's last:

'Okay, all for one and one for all and all that. Remind me, D'Artagnan, which ones get killed in the end?'

We talked for several hours; there were arguments over what was important and what wasn't, what we could do and what we should do. No-one asked the big question; what was 'Smokescreen?' Was it something political? Was it a smokescreen? I had a headache. The bottle stayed on the dining room table. The only thing we agreed was that we had to have an idea what 'Smokescreen' was:

'I've got an idea,' Little Mac hadn't offered much until this.

'Out with it then,' his sister said. I shot her a look. She shrugged.

'What I think we should do is this...'

Chapter 24

Friday the 13th of Groundhog

Next day, Grant and I turned in at CID, my report on McCrackers was done. Including a copy for me. There would be fallout from that; with luck I wouldn't see it. I was waiting for a phone call; the last piece before we'd try to build a better mousetrap. I was thinking about my dad, who'd liked the Kinks, but loved the Stones. On my 18th birthday he'd given me a CD and an 18 year old malt. I'd opened the CD: the Stones' Sticky Fingers. He'd read my face easily:

'Not your thing?'

'They're pathetic dad, poncing about on stage singing 25-year-old songs: they could be in Sunseeker motor cruisers and watching their polo ponies.'

'They do.'

'Even worse, so why bother?'

'People don't go to see them because of what they do, son, it's because of what they did. Nostalgia's something old people catch. Give it a listen. You might be surprised.'

I'd made to open the malt. He'd held up a hand. Licked his lips with a dry-looking tongue:

'Save that, for another day.' I noticed the tremor in the hand as he said it.

I often wondered what he have bought me on my 19th, if he'd lived to see it.

I did give it a listen, after 3 or 4 times I found I liked it. Particularly one song. When I started seeing Yol, a couple of years later, I'd played her the song; tried to make it 'Our Song'. It *wasn't* her thing. But I would play it after a fight, an aural white flag or request for parley. The song had only good memories for me; the CD was in the pile on the floor of the house in Northwood.

My head jerked as the phone rang, eyes swivelled to look at me; Off-Cut, Fritz, Ari and Grant's. Grant showed me some crossed fingers. Fritz shook an open fist in the universal male lack-of-bonding sign.

'Hello, DI Murray?'

'It's Jean. Yol called, there's a message for you.'

'What is it?' I said as patiently as I could.

'It's a bit odd, she said you'd know what it meant. She said tell him not to forget what comes next.'

'What...' I took a breath. 'Is it?'

'Wild Horses.' She hung up.

I gave Grant the thumbs-up, but then I couldn't help remembering that – like the saying goes – the lyrics continued 'couldn't drag me away.'

I got up from my seat, walked over to my ex-friend, Ari, and gave him the Glasgow kiss. His nose split, I had the satisfaction of seeing the gleam of cartilage amongst the red. Fritz and Off-Cut grabbed me:

'You won't get away with it! I've got evidence, you'll never find it. I'm taking it to the press.'

'Whad doo talkig aboud?' Ari was holding a handkerchief to his stricken nose.

'I've got it all, you bastard. Everything.' I hoped he wouldn't ask me what it was.

He shouted over to Grant:

'Phode the ACC, Elvis, the dubber's od by desk.' It would be, I thought.

'Which one? Mobile or office?' Grant asked.

'Which ebber one he adswers, stupid bitch!'

Her mouth tightened and she did as she was told.

'He's in the building, he said he'd be right down.'

Elvis breezed in, the expression on his face that of someone enjoying the best of days. He rubbed his hands together, smacked his lips:

'Now, what's all this Murray?'

I cocked the brow of a swollen eye at him; Ari's retribution had been taken in the time it took Elvis to negotiate the stairs.

'I've got stuff, I said. Anything happens to me, it'll go public.'

'I expect you have very little in fact. Your family safely out of the country now, I suppose? I thought you would get that news later rather than sooner, Murray. No matter.'

He sighed, shook his head; 'Well, what to do? We only need him out of the way for a while, after all.'

He was talking to himself, as visionaries do, I suppose: Fritz, Off-Cut and Ari were nodding anyway. Three men trying to appear wise.

'Yes, Murray. We have just the place for you. Yes we do.'

Elvis took out his mobile, pushed a button; speed dial. Funny how his mobile always worked.

'Mac, it's me.' He didn't put the call on loudspeaker.

'No, no, nothing like that. It's Murray: what we thought.' He listened, frowning.

'Yeah, I'd like to as well. Only he's on about evidence, if something happens to him... Usual daft threats. Could be a bluff.'

He waited. The wait seemed longer for me.

'Right, okay. Maybe that's best.'

I'd been paying too much attention to Elvis. He nodded. Everything went black.

I only ever found one thing worse than a hangover: concussion. You'd get everything but the high of the night before. If it was bad enough, you'd puke. I did. I just managed to roll onto my side and vomit over the side of the high bed. It was difficult in a strait-jacket. I looked at the bars on the windows and the heavy metal door. The jacket was definitely overkill. We'd built a better mousetrap then. Only thing was, was I the cheese or the mouse?

There must have been someone outside: I'd just finished retching when the door opened. All the medical paraphernalia was beside the bed: stand with drip, monitors, bed pan, cardboard urine bottle. I wasn't wired up. Not yet. The man in the white tunic looked more like a goon than a nurse. Big guy, then again if I was where I thought I was. They'd all be big. The slab of a man said nothing, maybe he couldn't speak. He pressed a big red button on the wall by the bed head. He remained hovering by the bed until the doctor came.

The haircut was severe, number two cut; a silver streak in the centre hadn't quite been eradicated. The pebble-lensed glasses did the doctor no favours in the looks department. I appreciated her figure though, even in the white coat. I didn't appreciate the needle she got out of a drawer in the trolley beside the bed. I was amazed when the accent was a Black Country burr instead of a teutonic consonant mangler.

'You just relax, this won't hurt a bit.'

It didn't; it hurt a lot.

'When you're quite relaxed, we can begin.'

It was nice, whatever it was... A four-pint feeling, only I didn't need a piss. An hour passed. Or a minute. The silent Golem removed the strait-jacket, my arms hung uselessly at my sides, numb.

'What is your name?' She said from a chair by my bed.

'Raymond Chandler Murray.' She ticked a box on a form.

I let out a giggle, and looked at her legs.

'What is your profession?'

'I am a policeman. I am the law. I am the strong man prepared to do violence that ye may creep into beds...'

The laughter sounded loony. Maybe it was the real me.

'What day is it?'

'Friday the 13th of Groundhog.'

I started barking like a dog. It seemed like a good idea, right then.

Ari appeared at the door, on his way somewhere else it seemed. The doctor leapt from the seat buttonholing him:

'You cretin, why didn't you say this man is an alcoholic. I'm wasting my time.'

As she and the Golem left shutting the security door behind them, I was howling like a lonely dog:

'My name is Raymond Chandler Murray and I'm an alcoholic.'

But I noticed the strait-jacket was still on the bed and not on me.

It took four hours for the drug, whatever it was, to wear off. At the sound of the key in the door, I decided to stay hop-happy for the benefit of the incoming audience.

The silent giant came in.

"Ware the Golem, Unbelievers!' I was pretty sure that was from a film.

He still didn't speak, just shook his head, laid a tray with a plastic bowl and spoon on the bedside table. I crooked a finger at him:

'BOO!' I shouted and gave someone the Glasgow kiss for the second time in 24 hours.

He made a wheezing noise and went down easily for such a big man. Poor quality clay. I smashed him over the head with a metal bed pan to put him out cold and took his tunic off him. I didn't let him freeze, I let him have the strait-jacket instead. I took his shoes, small for such a big man, they were still too big for my feet. They were more convincing than a barefoot mental nurse. Thank God I'd still had my own trousers.

I locked the door with the fallen giant's keys. A card in a slot beside the door had 'Special: Smokescreen' written on it. Safer than a name. The corridor still had the furnishings and once modishly tasteful pictures of the institution's former life as a rehabilitation centre for famous inadequates. All I needed to do was look for a card similar to the one outside my room. Easy.

Only it wasn't: easy. About every fifth door had a card similar to the one outside my 'private ward'. Strait-jackets, what looked like motorcycle crash helmets and a smattering of Lecter masks greeted me as I looked through the Judas Holes in the doors. It looked like a genuine equal opportunity operation, male, female, black, white, young, old. There were 20 doors to check. On this wing.

I prayed I'd be lucky. Someone would miss the Golem eventually, if not his conversation.

Room number CI, Roman numerals: a hangover from some prick's idea of lending class to the Priory in its 'inglory' days of popstars, poseurs and pathetic adulation junkies paying the price of fame. I opened the hatch. A fifty-something guy; took me a minute or two to recognise him. The wire-wool helmet hadn't been a wig after all. It looked a bit ragged, but then a strait-jacket didn't allow the brushing of one's hair. I caught his rolling, over-bright eye: he yelled in a familiar, hectoring voice:

'Your starter for ten on 19th century philosophy, give me the name of the 19th century movement whose main plank was the concept of 'the greatest good for the greatest number.''

He made a buzzing sound.

He looked me in the eye.

'University of Westminster, Blair?'

I turned away; left the hatch open: his voice carried through it as I continued down the corridor:

'COME ON! COME ON! Surely you know this...'

The die showed six for once. Two doors down Jackie Carlton, no strait-jacket but dull-eyed, was lying on the bed. I shook her, although she was sort of awake.

'We haven't got long.'

'Call me Jackie.' I hadn't called her anything.

'Why are you in here?'

'The government knows best.'

It came out as 'gommint' like a five-year-old's attempt at a word newly learned. Tranq-ed up way above the eyeballs.

'Yes, but why you?'

'Naturally, we need to protect the public. Not least from themselves.'

'Do you know something? Something dangerous?'

'Those opposing the government are by extension outside the norm. Suffering from delusion, or mental impairment.'

'What is Smokescreen?'

'If we rejoin Europe and reimplement Schengen, the movement of valued citizens will be more than the country can bear. We cannot allow the New Europeans to stride still further ahead of our great country.'

'What's this got to do with me?'

'We expect an initial flood out, out of the country. We need a distraction while we take the necessary steps. This government has never shirked from the difficult decision. When the camps are open the flood will stop. Once we control the flow'.

It sounded like a lunatic's manifesto, or a career ending speech, not like her end of our conversation. In any event, I had no clue what it meant. And she seemed unlikely to help us, even if we got her out. I locked her room. Went back to mine at a run. If the Golem had been missed...well, I didn't fancy my chances with Mengele's great grand-daughter.

The huge man was still out for the count. Maybe I'd killed him. Too bad. I stood by the wall, next to the door. Of course it opened outwards, so it wouldn't hide me when it did. But staying out of the sight-line was important, it would buy a second or two. After that, it would depend who came through the door.

I probably didn't wait long. Of course, it seemed like it. Finally the door opened. The scary doctor woman was speaking:

'Most irregular; the project associated patients rarely leave. In fact, I can't remember one.'

Another female voice:

'Yes, well, needs must. The Leader wants him. Now. And the other one.'

Grant's voice had the demagogic ring of Uncle Mac's: maybe the charisma came with the looks.

The plain face behind the pebble glasses contorted in a shriek. Grant cut her off with a downward blow of a handgun that had appeared in her fist.

'Quick, get out, get her keys.' She said.

'I've got his.' I pointed to the still inert mound on the floor.

'Let's get her.'

'Not sure she'll be much use.'

'It's the plan. Let's stick to it.'

'There's always plan B.'

'Not in my experience. Look, we haven't got time to argue.'

I thought I might have created CID's latest monster. But she was right; there wasn't time. We needed to get out.

At the access to this wing, Woodbine was tidying up. I couldn't see blood, but two or three clones of the giant in my room were being neatly arranged on the floor. Woodbine saw us:

'Fucking hurry up, can't you!' He shouted, a vibrato betraying the adrenalin, or panic, as it would have been in my case.

Jackie Carlton, was dead weight; still mumbling the kind of nonsense she'd been saying to me. Grant took over, Woodbine got me in an arm-lock: 'Got to be convincing, Murray. Might give it a tweak on the way out.' He laughed.

The tweak came as we passed reception. I said my line: 'Owww!'

Grant said to the receptionist: 'Doctor Reifenstahl wished to see another patient. She asked me to tell you she may be some time.'

That was more or less in the script. I hoped it hadn't been overwritten.

Little Mac was at the wheel of the Focus. Not the only unconvincing aspect of our operation, the car. We tried to look like undesirables being loaded into the car by Woodbine the minder. Our acting was probably below porno standard. As Little Mac drove off, I asked them;

'It was the magic word that did it, right?'

'Yep.'

'Yeah.'

'Of course.'

They all spoke at once, the euphoria of having pulled it off.

As we were waved out by the guards at the gate, I said:

'It's hard to see what's really going on behind a smokescreen.'

As we pulled into Little Mac's Soho street, the fire engine was the first thing we noticed. The blackened shell of the corner building was the second. Little Mac spoke first: 'Reckon he got out?'

'He's tougher than he looks.' I said, but I thought he might have really blown the looking after himself this time.

Two plods started to approach us, palm out in the international floor the accelerator sign. Little Mac did. The uniforms scurried to the safety of the pavements. The unlucky one was clipped by the front wing and fell into a junk shop window. Maybe the alarm shocked him more than the cuts from the glass.

'Where to?' Little Mac said. Over his shoulder, at me.

'Brixton.' Woodbine answered him.

Grant raised her eyebrows: 'You sure?'

'There are other passwords.' Woodbine said, and I thought that might be gnomic enough for Needles, wherever he was.

Chapter 25

Safe House

The needle was at 65 in Brick Lane, the shops were empty; despite the jagged teeth of the remaining glass in the windows, all the goods had been liberated years ago. The alien script on the signs was as meaningless to us as to the rumoured residents. Maybe it was an urban myth: a community of underclass rejects, living by mugging for human organs. People spoke about the Surgeon in whispers. It was a name that never appeared in the papers. The Lane wasn't policed at all, never mind after dark.

'Stop the car! Do you know who I am?' It was the former ForSec.

'We do,' I said. 'I doubt your constituents would recognise you though.'

'Who the fuck are you?'

'That depends,' Little Mac said.

She sat back between Woodbine and I. Trying to work out how she'd got there.

Everyone was quiet as we pulled into the Loughborough Estate. Woodbine directed Little Mac to a low-rise with every other front door missing. Woodbine got out:

'Whatever happens, stay with the car.'

He went into the main entrance. A few minutes later he appeared on the 2nd floor, checking the numbers where there were doors. He knocked at the 7th door down. It looked like he was pulled in.

The politician was starting to look more human. She went for the door handle. Thought better of it. Grant opened her handbag, handed the politico a compact and a comb. Jackie Carlton opened the compact first. Her eyes went wide as she looked into it. She attacked her hair with the comb. Four strokes later the comb was completely jammed. She dropped her hands helplessly into her lap. I untangled the comb, and began restoring some order to her hair. She let me.

Little Mac adopted a cockney accent as bad as Dick Van Dyke's:

'I 'ad that Jackie Carlton in the back o'me cab...'

'Shut the fuck up!' Grant said.

It became a little darker in the car. 5 or 6 boys, teenagers, or young men were peering through the windows. I heard the click of the central locking. They did nothing. Didn't touch the car. They merely made room as more boys joined them: every so often stepping aside to allow the newcomers their turn at peering in.

'How long as he been?' Little Mac's eyes darted from shadowy figure to shadowy figure outside the car's cocoon.

Grant looked at her watch: 'Fifteen minutes.'

'Seems longer,' her brother grunted.

'Time is relative.' The politico said.

'The perception of time is ultimately an incoherent illusion.' I countered.

'And where did you learn that bollox?' Grant snorted.

'I read it on a beer mat once.'

Woodbine Moses-ed the sea of disaffected youth around the car. Or maybe that was the guy with him. 6 feet 6, he was sporting dreadlocks, a rare sight, even there. Woodbine rapped on the window.

'Come on, follow me.'

We did. Up to the second floor, through the 7th door down. It opened into a wreck of a front room. Rubbish tip furniture surrounded by rubbish hiding whatever floorcovering we couldn't see. The dreadlocks took out a bunch of keys, opened six locks on a very heavy door on the back wall. We trooped through, and Dreadlocks drew up the drawbridge behind us.

There wasn't the half-expected rabbit-down-the-hole moment: the room looked remarkably similar to the one we'd just left. Except for the cartoon safe. It should have had 'ACME' in big letters on the front. It looked old and very heavy. It stood taller than Dreadlocks. Woodbine pointed at him, then at the metal monstrosity:

'Vic says we can use the safe too, for the disks and the tape, whatever.'

'Should be safe enough.' I said.

He went on, 'We'll be OK here, I don't think they'll find us. I've used it before. It's our place, when you need to keep something or someone out of circulation.'

'I get it, a Safe House.' The joke fell flat, maybe because we were in one.

Vic tossed Woodbine the keys: they did the daft handshake, high-five crap. I suspected it was for our benefit. Vic left and Woodbine re-secured the door. We took our chances on the mis-matched totters'-reject furniture. It was time. Jackie Carlton looked awake enough. I nodded at Grant: she spoke.

'Foreign Sec-'

'Call me Jac-'

'Give that shit up!' I cut her off: Call me Jeff; bad cop. Grant Mutt-ed up:

'Ms Carlton, why were you in the Clinic? Did you check yourself in?'

The hazel eyes darted from side to side, took refuge in the ragged lampshade above our heads.

'I'm not sure. Do I know you two?'

'We've met recently, Ms Carlton. How do you mean you're not sure?'

'I did PM's questions; they broke off during them. Then I was in the lobby.'

Predictably her hand went to her mouth. She looked from me to Grant, and back.

'Yes, it was us.' I sneered.

'So what happened, next, Ms Carlton?'

'You've seen it.' She looked horrified.

'It wasn't that bad. At least it isn't on the Internet like it would have been a few years ago. No, it wasn't bad at all.' I gave her a leer for good measure.

She went for a slap. Woodbine's strong hand grabbed her wrist.

'The CCTV doesn't concern us now.' Grant snapped it out. She probably thought I'd overdone it.

'Kilgour and one of his cronies took me to a room to lie down. It was a shock.'

I couldn't resist: 'Why! You twats are responsible for recording more video than any government in the world, ARE YOU THICK!'

My spittle landed on her cheek and this time Little Mac's hand restrained me.

'I'm OK, I'm OK!' I shook him off.

Grant nodded at Woodbine and said:

'See if you can find him something to drink.'

'I said I'm OK.'

Grant looked at me for a second or two, then turned to the woman:

'So, Jackie, if you really do prefer that, what happened then?'

'I lay down. Kilgour got me a drink, brandy. I don't like brandy but he insisted.'

'Is that the last thing you remember before..?'

'I remember a hospital room, private not NHS. A needle, needles. I think I saw him, but it might have been a nightmare.'

Naturally, she was pointing at me.

Woodbine shoved a chunky shot glass in my hand: I smelled coconut. Took a drink of the clear fluid. Malibu. Neat. Woodbine laughed and shrugged his shoulders. I tossed the rest off and handed him the glass.

'So. Jackie. Why did they lock you up? Why not a convenient accident? Like our dear departed PM.' My smile was probably as nasty as my breath.

She stiffened her spine, the sofa creaked: 'You saw the footage, it really was an accident.'

'Jackie,' Grant put a hand on hers: 'We recovered the time stamp data.'

The spine turned to jelly. Her head was in her hands.

'You saw. He was dead. I didn't know what to do. I called Kilgour, Mac. He was there in 20 minutes. Checked the pulse, there was nothing we could do. Nothing.'

'You must have done something. What did you do with him for 2 days?'

Grant's voice was metallic.

'Mac took care of it. Said he'd put him on ice for a couple of days, while he made a plan. Such a waste.'

'Why?' She flinched as I spoke.

'Because he'd decided, we were going back in. The European Union. Only this time it was all the way: Schengen, CEP and the Euro.'

'So? Why didn't we? Why didn't you?' I asked.

But Little Mac answered: 'He told you he had the CCTV vid, didn't he?'

'Yes, he did. And I went along with it. At first. On the morning of PM's Questions I told him I'd get it through Parliament and take my chances on the video.'

Grant and I looked at each other.

'And he tried to force the issue with that Windbag's question.,' Grant said.

I nodded at her: 'Kilgour must have been overjoyed at our performance. Absolutely made up.'

I wanted to spit the dry, bitter taste out of my mouth.

'Hey, Woodbine.' I said. 'See if you can find something less paradise cocktail to drink. I need a nightcap.'

Chapter 26

"So's smoking"

I woke up leaning against the back of one of the sofas. An empty half-bottle of cherry brandy in my left hand. Grant was still managing to look half-decent in spite of the absence of her magic suitcase. Jackie Carlton looked like what she was: a middle-aged woman overtaken by events. We'd backed a rank outsider and no mistake. Over at the window, I cleared some filthy condensation with the elbow of my jacket. Daylight. 5 or 6 slim figures circled the Focus. On guard or in wait: I couldn't tell.

We left the filthy flat. Woodbine stayed behind to make the safe room secure. We got the dead-eyed look from the young men by the car, until they scattered when Woodbine caught us up. The others looked at me expectantly:

'What?' I said.

'We thought there might be a plan, Guv!' Grant used the title for the first time in days.

'A plan? You want a fuckin' plan! I'm not even sure what's happened so far, how do you expect me to know what to do next?'

'We don't have anything really, do we?' Grant sounded sad.

Little Mac cleared his throat: 'There's nothing to tie Uncle Mac to any of this.'

I turned on him: 'I expect you're pretty pleased about that, eh?'

His lower lip came out: 'No... anyway, that's what we need to do, isn't it?'

'But how?' was Jackie Carlton's contribution.

'Just get in the car,' I said.

'Use your contacts, threaten, beat, shoot them, if you have to: just find out what happened to Needles,' I said to Woodbine through the open window, as the three of us and Little Mac left in the car.

'Big haystack, London,' he called out, as Little Mac drove off.

Jackie Carlton, Grant and I had been dropped off 200 yards from our nick. I wanted a car. Couldn't think where else to get one. I just hoped we could avoid Fritz and the gang, while we got it. Grant told the other woman to wait by the lamp-post outside the laundrette. The station yard was empty of people. I pointed at the car Ari Chryssipous and I had shared for five years. Grant nodded. I smiled as I opened the door. Pulling the ignition key from the not-quite pristine ashtray, I reflected that old habits died hard. I stood up sharply, almost banging my head on the passenger door frame. It might have hurt less than the gun barrel in my back.

'Ray, Ray. You are just so predictable. Turn round, carefully now'

The gold tooth glinted in Ari's mouth. I longed to practise some gulag dentistry on it.

'Good boy. Bet you don't hear that often, nowadays.'

'Bet you do.'

He gave me a tap on my cheek with the barrel of the gun.

'Be nice, Ray. Where are the others?'

'Well one of them's behind you.'

Ari laughed. 'Remember those TV cop shows, they were so funny. Just like you, Ray.'

His eyes bulged when Grant's own gun smashed into the back of his skull. I gave him a kick on his way down.

'Sometimes I kill myself.' I said.

We picked up Carlton. In another part of town not too far away, someone would have already done it. As bad as she looked.

'Northwood.' I told Grant.

'Again?'

'I need to see my sister-in-law.'

'The SOCO?'

'I don't have any others.'

Jean Okocha lived three streets from my recently marketed home. I hadn't stepped across her threshold... well, in almost five years. If she wasn't in, so be it, we'd wait. Not even she worked all day, every day – however often I'd bumped into her recently. Her street looked reasonable: rubbish was piled neatly, the blind windows were crisply boarded-up. There was almost no grafitti. A nice middle-class area. I banged on the door. Her partner answered immediately.

'Ray, what...' she shook her head as if not quite believing my presence on her doorstep.

'Ruth, I ... we need to see Jean. Can we wait inside?'

She looked over my shoulder and her mouth opened in an O of surprise: she pointed:

'That's... that's...' She couldn't get it out, but not because she couldn't remember.

'Yeah, it is. And that's why we need to get off the streets.'

We barged past her, the mouth still working like a gasping fish's.

Inside it was as chintzy as old Miss McCracken's. Gilt ornaments, knick-knacks everywhere, antimacassars on the chair backs. What the fuck was a macassar? A disease? A Turkish soldier? The decor was bizarre enough taken on its own: the first time I'd been in this house had been the second time I'd seen Jean and Ruth together. Ruth's taste in clothes ran to leopardskin prints and not much further. Jean wore smart, practical, tailored suits: because of her job as a SOCO and pulling those white noddy suits on and off. Weird.

We sat: Grant was keeping Jackie Carlton on a close rein, guiding the politico into the 2-seat cottage suite sofa beside her. I sat in one of the chairs. I was glad. We'd covered up three-quarters of the floral pattern; it had been hurting my eyes.

'Tea?' Ruth said stiffly.

'Not for me.' I said.

'She could be a while,' she said.

'What time are you expecting her?' Grant might have been making conversation.

'I see her when I see her, lately.'

And she swept out of the lounge, in a blur of yellow and black.

Grant whispered hoarsely to me:

'What the fuck are we doing here? We're eyebrows deep in shit and you're visiting relatives? What are you doing?'

'Wait and see.' I said, although I wasn't sure I actually knew.

The tea came, ours was weak in mismatched 'humourous' mugs. Mine said 'world's greatest lover', Grant smirked when I held it up for her to look. Hers was about fish and bicycles. We both knew who held the truth in their hands. The politico's hands were clasped completely round her mug, treasuring the warmth, although the house wasn't cold. Ruth's mug was completely plain:

'You OK, Ray?' Grant had her head to one side, as if talking to a child or a dog.

'What?'

She nodded down towards my foot, it looked like a rock drummer's on the bass pedal. I couldn't stop it for a few seconds. Grant spoke again:

'When did you last have a smoke?'

'What? Last one, a couple of days ago: outside the Number 6. Why?'

'Your finger ends are bleeding.' I looked at my nails. I hadn't realised I'd been doing that either. Grant tossed me a rectangular packet, too small for cigarettes. The packaging was completely blank. Cellophane wrapped. I struggled to open it, dropped it twice.

'What the fuck is it anyway?'

'Nicotine gum: Uncle Mac...'

'Yeah, yeah. Good old Uncle.' I snarled.

'They're all on it. See them on the TV in the House, all trying not to chew if they see the camera on them.'

'You used to smoke then?' I asked, popping two pieces in and waiting for the rush.

'I quit a long time ago. They're just a security blanket really. I don't need them.'

'That long, eh?

'A lifetime ago.'

'When though?'

I spilled some of the tea as I leaned forward. Surprisingly it was just strong enough to make it to the carpet. Ruth flicked a hand, shrugged.

'About three weeks before the abortion.' Grant said.

The tea was already cold, but I drank it.

About 5 in the afternoon, we heard the key in the door. No-one moved. Not even Ruth. Jean walked in. Out of her white SOCO gear, she looked so like her sister.

'Oh...' It was half way between a cough and a gasp.

'I needed to see you.' I said.

'Look, Ray. I don't know anything else. I gave you the message.'

'It's not about Yol. I need to know something. About the PM's death.'

She looked at Ruth for the first time. Her lover's shoulders dropped and she looked for something in the whorls of the carpet.

'What?' Jean said.

I stood up. Tried for eye contact and got it. She was chin-up, steady-eyed.

'Who did the SOCO's job on the PM?'

'You were there, you saw me.'

'No, where the body was found.'

The chin dropped a little.

'Just fucking tell him.' It was Ruth, still searching the Axminster.

'I did it.'

'Another favour.' It was a statement.

She shook her head: 'You haven't a fucking clue have you?'

'What I really want know is, who pronounced him dead at the scene that wasn't the scene? Not Harbottle?'

'See what I mean? No, it wasn't Harbottle. It was your wife.'

'Don't talk daft. She's a fucking GP.'

She laughed: 'One of your bosses, the one you don't like, looks like a parade-ground policeman. Enjoys the uniform. He brought her to the scene.'

'Elvis.' I said. Name the demon.

'Why her?'

'They keep files on everyone, especially the people trying to get out. Do you really think they don't care who goes back to Nigeria?'

'But still, why her?'

'I don't know. Wild coincidence happens in crime novels, why not in real life? Anyway, if she wanted to get out, she had to do what they said.'

'What about you?'

'Are you really that stupid? I'm going too, as soon as I get a ticket.'

I noticed she hadn't said we're going. Ruth looked up from the carpet at last:

'Is that it, then? Will you go now?'

Grant stepped in: 'The minister and I would like to borrow some clothes. We really need to change. A shower? Please.'

Yol barked a laugh: 'Sure, make yourselves at home, it's just the minister's more Ruth's size than mine.'

Jean went upstairs to sort the women out with some clothes, while they showered. Ruth still sat in the chair, still fascinated by her own taste in floorcoverings.

'Not going with her, then?'

'No. I could though. I came up on the White Card lottery. Just...'

'Not for you?'

'It's hard to explain. I don't want to be an immigrant; we've been together years. She still gets the look. You must know that. They were born here, your wife and Jean... I couldn't have stood it.'

'It's against the law, Ruth.'

She laughed; a bitter, wintry sound : 'So's smoking, Ray.'

Chapter 27

Sergeant Major Cousins

It was quiet in the car. I hadn't heard a word out of the politico for hours. Grant was just driving aimlessly, like I'd told her to. I needed to think. My phone beeped. It was a message. Another from beyond the grave, perhaps. Needles number was showing as the sender. I read it out:

'12.00 : got something. Off to King's X. Meet with ex-army Sgt Cousins.'

'Maybe he's still alive.' Grant offered.

'We'd know for sure if he'd put a date on it.'

'Army?'

It was Jackie. Looking a little better for the shower but maybe not the leopard skin blouse and the barmaid-cut skirt.

'That's what it said.'

'It'll be a down-and-out, at King's Cross. Maybe a druggie. Certainly an alkie, if not. Hardly likely to be much use, an alcoholic?'

Her smile would have cut me to the quick if I'd given a shit what a politician thought.

'Right. Let's make for the Loughborough. If Woodbine's on time, we'll only have to wait 10 minutes.'

It wasn't the best of decisions. The youths surrounded the car within seconds. The first few minutes they eyeballed us through the glass. I mimed yawning at them. It became less boring. Two of them ran off somewhere: the rest began rocking the car.

I really did hope Woodbine would be on time. The car stopped rocking. The kids backed off. Liquid splashed on the windscreen first. The two youths had come back with jerry-cans, the liquid was splashing liberally on the sides, the roof, the boot. We flinched at the clang of the cans' being discarded. The car was surrounded again: they were doing the rock-concert lighter waving thing, although I doubted their tastes ran to that kind of music.

Finally, the Focus screeched up. The gang drew back, flames still wounding the night. We got out; Woodbine shoo'd the gang off.

I turned to the women: 'Smell that?'

'I can't smell anything.' The politician said.

'Me neither,' said Grant.

I touched a finger to the roof, licked the liquid from my skin.

'Water. Never touch the stuff.' I said.

Inside the safe room, we discussed our respective progress. It felt more like a police operation than anything I'd done in years. When Grant had finished debriefing our day, Little Mac said:

'Still, I don't think it's enough. Even if we had Needles to get the story out. And the other stuff, Me and Sis... Well it's he said she said, isn't it? Who will people believe?'

'You've got a self-esteem problem, Little Mac, if you think you're less credible than a politician.'

Our pet politician kept her mouth shut. The only time I would ever trust what an honorable member said. But I knew what Little Mac meant, sometimes it was easier to believe as you were told.

'What about Needles?' Grant asked Woodbine.

'There isn't much. He was seen in King's Cross, talking to the dossers, day before yesterday. About midday.'

'They know where he went?'

'It was dossers he was talking to, Murray. We're lucky they remembered he was there.'

'You've nothing more?'

'He was seen near Little Mac's place later that afternoon, that's all.'

'Doesn't look good for Needles,' I said.

I turned to Jackie Carlton, in her marginal-taste clothes:

'What's with the curfew? There are soldiers on the streets, sure: but it seems easy enough to avoid them. We've been out after dark pretty much as we like.'

'The troops are partly for show, partly for some construction work. The ones in London are at St Pancras and Paddington.'

'What are they building?' Grant examined her nails, still a perfect manicure.

'Extra platforms for hi-speed links. Dover and Heathrow.'

'Why?' Little Mac seemed intrigued. Woodbine stifled a yawn.

'I can't work it out.' Carlton shrugged; 'It was an initiative the late PM was really keen on: connected with getting back into Europe. The Leader is following through for reasons of his own.'

'So we can probably break the curfew whatever?'

'If you can avoid the trouble. Civil disturbances.'

'What? A few white supremacists, beating up teenagers?' I sneered.

'Ah,' was her less than illuminating reply.

Grant stood up, brushed down the pants of my sister-in-law's tailored black suit. It was a good fit. I checked the fit out thoroughly as she walked over to where the politician sat on the tired sofa. I flinched on hearing the contact of palm with skin.

'What is Smokescreen?' Grant sounded mean. I'd have answered.

'Grant is au fait with all modern police methods, as you can see, minister. Why don't you answer the nice lady?'

She coloured up, looked from Woodbine to Little Mac, cleared her throat: 'I- I'm not sure. I mean... I'm not really in the Leader's Gang.'

I almost wished Harry Xeno had been there so I could whistle a few bars of Gary Glitter.

Grant puffed out her cheeks: 'Just tell us what you think then.'

'They're not going into the EU. I know that much, but I think they might want the public to think so. The only other thing I've heard is something about 'Camps.' That's all.'

'Not much, is it.' Grant said.

'No,' I said. 'We've still got the dosser's name from Needles' message. King's Cross tomorrow for us, Grant.'

'What about us?' Woodbine said. Little Mac nodded his inclusion.

I pointed at the MP. 'Babysitting.'

She said something anatomical under her breath.

For once, I went to sleep, rather than passing out. We'd let the women have the sofas. Grant had protested longer than the politician did. Little Mac and Woodbine took a chair each, and I made my acquaintance with yet another floor. Not the worst, not the best. I caught the faint whiff of stale ash as I dropped off. Maybe that accounted for the tobacco dreams.

It was smokey. A room I recognised and couldn't quite place. And I mean smokey. There *was* someone smoking; just one person producing a fug of dry ice proportions. They were a silhouette: a huge searchlight back-lit them, and the fug. They were smoking a Holmes-ian pipe. I could hear martial music. It drowned out what the person was saying. The room disappeared, the searchlight stayed. The music was drowned out by the rushing sound of a train's arrival. Loudspeaker announcements bellowed indistinctly, the echo undiminished in repetition. The train pulled away, the figure started to come through the smoke, I couldn't hear words but I had the impression of a strong woman's voice.

Then:

'Come on, come on.'

It was Jackie Carlton, shaking me awake, a little more violently than I'd have liked.

'You were raving. Grant told me to wake you. Bad dream?'

'I don't know. I think I prefer alcohol induced dreams. Those make more sense.'

But I wished the figure behind the smokescreen had shown itself before she woke me up.

Jackie Carlton's outfit hat not suffered too much for her night on the sofa. The violent print of the blouse hid a multitude of wrinkles, and the skirt was too tight to wrinkle at all. The shoes were her own.

It surprised me how little they jarred with the rest of her borrowed ensemble. Still, she'd had a similar pair on in the CCTV footage. For once, Grant looked slightly less than perfect, a crease or two behind the knees of Jean Okocha's trousers. I wondered where she kept the make-up bag.

Woodbine said: 'I'm not happy about the babysitting, Murray. I need a shower and a change of clothes, and I can't get either here.'

'You're not dumping her on me.' I saw Little Mac's bottom lip once again.

'I am here, you know.' The 'baby' said.

'I really don't give a fuck if you go for a spa treatment and a tailor's appointment. Just take the cow with you.'

My voice was trying for a hiss, but my mouth was so dry it came out like a croak.

'Do we get the car?' Little Mac asked.

'There are two, aren't there?' I was contemplating another glass of the malibu.

'I meant the swine saloon.' He said.

'Yeah, whatever. We'll take the gun from the boot though.'

The Focus was suffering from an overdose of noughts. The clock had gone round; or the car had been driven for 10 miles a year for the last 15. It would have run a bit better if that were the case. It was okay for running over an overweight plod, but not for outrunning even the pathetic unmarked we'd let Little Mac have. But at least it was identifiably *not* a police car. The dents and rust spots were absent on mine and Ari's old car: essential maintenance and servicing of the Met's fleet had finally improved once they'd realised the cars wouldn't be replaced every 2 years. Naturally, Grant was driving: I had the last of the Malibu in my pocket just in case. She looked over at me. It was going to be Matron's hygiene lecture again:

'You could go another shower, yourself. And a change of clothes.'

'To visit the homeless?'

'To avoid being mistaken for one of them. Anyway, I'm having a shower, whatever.'

'And where are you going to do that?'

'Wait and see. Shopping first.'

'With what?'

'I'll take care of it. You just stay in the car.'

Grant abandoned the car at the junction of Old Street and Whitecross Street in Islington. The market was a sad thing now. A flea market more or less. God knows what clothes she was going to bring back with her. Or how long it would take. It was a good job I hadn't ribbed her about the prospect. She returned with arms full of clothes and stowed them in the boot.

'I hope I'm colour-coordinated,' I said as she slid into the driver's seat.

For reply I got a look of contempt. It might have meant she would never mis-match colours, but I reckoned she just thought I was an arsehole. The malibu still tasted foul. I tried again.

'Don't suppose you got underwear?' This time she did laugh:

'That's why we're having a shower,' she stopped the car. 'It's commando for us, for the foreseeable.'

We were outside the Ironmonger Street Baths, we'd driven a scant few hundred meters down Old Street. She turned to me: 'I'm having the full turkish, soap, scrape and steam, the lot.'

'I want to get to that ex-serviceman...' it came out whiny.

'He'll keep. After all, where's he got to go?'

I did the full issue too. It was a mistake. I was embarrassed: at being naked in front of her, by so obviously not looking at her and by the DTs that sweating out the alcohol brought on. It felt odd afterwards; different, not better, just strange. I wished I had a toothbrush. We changed into some of the clothes she'd bought at Whitecross: I tried not to think of what was under hers. She strode to the car, her power-dresser suit looked like haute couture on her. I looked like a well-dressed scarecrow.

'King's Cross then,' She said, and she moved the car off while I looked at her legs.

It was unbelievable, we'd driven around London in the Focus for days and not been pulled once. A temporary barrier blocked our way. We'd have driven through it in the unmarked, if the plastic policemen hadn't moved it out of the way in time. But we were in the Focus. The unsmiling faces waved us over to the side of Farringdon Road.

These uniformed 'support staff' had never been smart, even when they first started to proliferate around the turn of the century. Now you could hardly tell the difference between them and the rip-off gangs who pulled Joe Public over and demanded on the spot fines. We were really unlucky. The road check was genuine. And we hadn't paid the congestion charge. People rarely did, you took a chance on the spot fine of £500. We showed our warrant cards, of course.

'Official business, Inspector?' The older, fatter one asked.

'Yes, exactly, now if you'll just-'

'Only, not an official vehicle this, sir, is it?'

The younger, acne-d one smirked, picked his ear and examined the wax.

'No but...'

'Well, you understand I'll have to fine you. But you'll get the receipt and can claim on expenses.'

He began writing out the ticket. Grant said: 'I'll just have to get some cash from the boot .'

Fatso almost dropped his pen as she gave him a bit of leg when she got out. Neither he nor Skinny complained as she bent over to search in the boot for a little longer than necessary. Fatso dropped the pen, his pad and his jaw as she pointed the pump action in their general direction. Skinny was immobilised, the little finger half way to his ear for a second mouthful.

'Get in there.'

She jerked the pump action at the plastic hut effort council workers had used to use to hide and drink tea in.

'Wait until you hear the car go. Then wait some more. Then wait a bit more, after that. Good boys'.

They did as they were told. Good job. She drove slowly away; one hand only on the wheel, the pump action steady at the hut until it didn't matter.

We pulled up outside the temporary fencing outside St Pancras. Army personnel were carrying building materials, driving machinery and a few held mobiles or radios to their ear. It looked busy, purposeful. We left the car and took the short walk to Kings Cross. The front was empty of toms in the early afternoon: as the clock hands advanced the homeless would move on, finally melting away to who knew where, leaving the night to the women brave or desperate enough to try and earn a living on the streets. The variety of the indigent still surprised me. Used to be ragged-haired shouters of either sex, carrying plastic bags or pushing trolleys. The demographic was very different now.

Whole families occasionally begged or busked on the crowded pavements. Some, especially middle-aged men, kept up pathetic attempts at personal grooming: the facial cuts and patchy bristle giving them away as they stepped closer. Appearances could be deceptive: often these were not the best sources of information. Still more often their grip on reality had slipped away with their self-respect. I looked at Grant,

'Pick a card, any card.'

'There must be hundreds of people.'

'So just pick one.'

She buttonholed a woman between 30 and 50 or 50 and 70, depending how long she'd lived on the street. I put her at the lower end, using the layers of clothes like the rings of a tree trunk to calculate her age.

'I'm looking for someone.' Grant said.

The woman smiled, showing a respectable number of teeth and I congratulated myself on my guess.

'Aren't we all, luv. Anyone in particular, or just Mr Right?'

'A former soldier, name of Cousins.'

The woman laughed : 'Names are for real people.'

'Never mind.' Grant started to turn away, stopped and slipped her a banknote.

'Ta, love. Look, ask people for the Sergeant Major. Could be him. Or he might know who you want, hey?'

We chose people at random, Grant slipped them all something. They must have thought she was Mother Teresa reincarnated. We stopped a ragged man from running away and recoiled from his breath as he rasped:

'What? I haven't done it, whatever it is!'

'We're just looking for someone, that's all.'

'I don't know him, I don't know anyone!'

The rapid movement of his eyes suited the nightmare his life had become. He wore a lot of clothes, very likely he was much thinner than the Michelin figure he cut. I thought he must be well on the way to seventy. I said carefully, clearly:

'We're looking for the Sergeant Major.'

The eyes locked into a steady gaze, he became around six inches taller. He must have just straightened up, but I didn't see him do it. His chest came out and his chin up, his very soul came on parade:

'25161970 Company Sergeant Major Cousins 2 Para, sir.'

He remained at attention, looked at me expectantly. I looked at Grant, who shrugged.

'Ah... Sergeant Major. Need some information. Could you oblige me? A few questions.'

'Yes sir, of course sir.'

'We're looking for a journalist. Sharp's the name.'

'Oh yes sir, I've seen him sir. It was...' I learned what crestfallen looked like.

'Not important, Sar'Major. Not important. You did see him though.'

'Oh yes sir.' He looked happier, on surer ground. 'Asked me about Goose Green. Made a tape. Said it was for a book. Did I do right sir?'

'You did very well, Sar'Major. What sort of questions?'

'He wanted to know about Captain Grant and Lieutenant Kilgour, sir.'

'What did you tell him?'

'The truth sir. He told me the Lieutenant had sent him. I know he's out now. An ex-serviceman like me. Can't get out of the habit though. Mr Kilgour it should be, I suppose.'

I rubbed my finger and thumb together and glanced at Grant. She gave me a banknote.

'One last thing, Sar'Major. Have a drink in the Mess on me.'

I gave a salute learned from the war movies, flicked a hand at an imaginary hat:

'Carry on Sergeant Major!' I said.

He returned the salute and executed a perfect quarter turn, before seeming to shrink before my eyes. We walked back to the car in silence.

'How did you know?' Grant asked me in the car.

'It was quite bad for my dad, just before the end. My dad's former company commander came to visit him. After the hospital had sent dad home. It went a bit like... like that did.'

I felt her looking at me. 'Just drive,' I said.

Chapter 28

"You public school fuckers"

I admit I was relieved to see the others' vehicle pulling into the Loughborough estate just before us. It was still light. Wouldn't be soon. Grant gave the horn a blast and I saw the figure in the back of their car jump a little. Served her right, she should have known it was us: I'd have expected her to be keeping an eye out once the car entered the Loughborough. We bailed out of the car. Followed the others up to the safe room. Woodbine had a plastic bag full of something, I could smell food. The others would be grateful, I supposed.

The food wasn't Chinese or Indian, or even Kebab: with dark approaching a visit to Soho or the Enclave would have been too time-consuming, and too dangerous. Woodbine piled food on a low coffee table: Polish kiełbasy, kołduny and zrazy: sausages, stuffed slices of beef and meat dumplings.

'Do you like this stuff?' I asked.

'It's what there is.' Woodbine said.

'Did you buy any drink?'

He reached into his leather jacket pocket, tossed me a half-bottle of Navy Rum.

Grant stayed my hand as it reached for the cap:

'Take what you need. And save some for later, too.'

'Thanks. I'll remember to wash behind my ears as well.'

She showed me her back as she turned towards the food. All of them set upon the Polish stuff like it was the last they'd ever see. At least it was edible with just your fingers. I leaned over Little Mac's shoulder and plucked a kielbasa, sat down with my sustenance on the sofa, while the others stood around the table, silently devouring their feast.

Woodbine smacked his lips, and told me to get up. I had to jump as he tipped the sofa onto its front. A full crate of Elephant Beer was just distinguishable in a pile of dust bunnies and paper wrappers. He handed round a bottle each:

'I do like Polish food as it happens, but it bloody makes me thirsty. Remember Zbigniew from school, Little Mac?'

'The jewboy?'

'Aww, that's shit, what did they call you, hey? Dirty Mac, wasn't it?'

'Yeah...I hated that name.'

'Exactly, you stupid bastard.'

I wondered what else the boarding school bullies used to call 'Carlton' Woodbine and if the cigarette nick-name had been kept simply because the other names had been altogether too predictably cruel. I enjoyed the beer even more than the rum, but then it was 7.2%, so it did the job. Grant said:

'What did you do today, bro?'

Woodbine gave her a sharp look, until Little Mac answered:

'We kept looking for Needles.'

'Any luck?' I said.

'Some.' Woodbine said.

'And?' I let him enjoy the moment.

'There's good news, bad news and worse news.'

'Come on, Woodbine.' Grant didn't.

'The good news is...'

'Fuck that, just get on with it!' Just the facts, sir, in modern police parlance.

So he did. Woodbine had looked up a friend in the fourth estate: Needles best pal as it happened. Joan Crow: a one time columnist for the Daily Express, I'd seen her from time to time in the Number Six, always someone blond and younger and far too handsome in tow. People said they were escorts; maybe they were. They earned their money after Joan's 7th double, when the foul-mouthed abuse started. Needles had said as far as Westminster went, she knew where all the corpses were interred. Bodies were for Whitehall to deal with, she reckoned. Crow said she'd put Needles onto the Sergeant Major:

'If he did get the story out of the deadbeat... well it's the only thing that fake Kilgour is bothered about. It's not really a rumour, just something whispered late at night, near the end of the bottle. Off the record of course, cheers.'

I watched Jackie Carlton's face as Woodbine related Crow's words: her eyes shone a little, recreating a little of her pre-upheaval persona. She ran her tongue across her lips, seemed about to speak. I held up a hand:

'Wait. She say what it was, Woodbine?'

'No, just Army stuff. Gave me some crappy quote, I think we had it in school.'

'What?'

'Unhappy the land that needs heroes.'

'Brecht.' The politician said. 'An unlikely writer for the Crow to quote.'

'Yeah, well. She say anything a bit more, like, useful?'

I flicked a dismissive hand at Jackie Carlton or at the literary crap, I wasn't sure which.

'Well, that's the...

'Yeah, yeah. Bad news. Enough, huh?'

'He's gone to ground, she reckons.'

'That's not so bad. Where?'

'That's the problem. Brick Lane.'

'She know where?'

'The old tube station.'

A grinning Mayor of London had renamed it 'Brick Lane' instead of Aldgate East, just in time for the Olympics. Within 18 months the area was abandoned by Sylhetis who retreated to the Enclave. So many South Asians longed for the 'good old days': before Iran, the oil crisis and the backlash against "Islamists" had made life impossible for anyone Asian no matter what their religion. It was sickening, how all the lip-service legislation in the world didn't change a thing. Not really, not deep down. Not people's fear of the other: atavistic, irrational - all those long words that my wife had used to try and explain people's reactions to us.

Grant and I exchanged a look. The politico, her voice slightly breathless, said:

'You're going, then. To find him.'

'I'm coming too.' Woodbine said. 'Safety in numbers.'

'Got a posse up your jumper?' I said, Grant gave me whack on the arm.

'Okay, okay.' I said. 'Thanks.'

Woodbine acknowledged it with a nod.

'Keep an eye on her.' Grant said over her shoulder to Little Mac, as we left.

There was more traffic than usual. The curfew, like so many things instituted by government in the last 20 years, was ineffective. Prohibition, the ban on smoking had been such a surprise; so many people just went along with it. Of course, Woodbine and Chryssipous and other criminals saw it as an opportunity: another commodity for the illegal market. I'd smoked some interesting stuff with my illegal snout over the last few years: dried banana skin, all sorts of herbal shite, the dried basil had made me sick. My former sidekick and I had unknowingly scored tobacco cut with skunk on one memorable occasion. Ari hadn't inhaled, thank goodness. I think it was the last day on the job I'd really enjoyed.

We took the police vehicle, although it wouldn't offer much protection in Brick Lane. It was faster, better maintained and Woodbine fit into it more easily. Outside the tube station looked deserted. The scuttle of rats or other unseen vermin the only sound. There were no street lights. I wished we had a torch. Carlton and I got out lighters, mine was a Zippo, I couldn't remember when I'd filled it last, or what with. It was still possible to access the
station, the open entryway was blocked only by the detritus common to all deserted slums. The usual inexplicable shopping trolleys, plastic bags and single shoes were all that hindered our progress.

'Down to the tracksides, or not?' Woodbine said.

'You know him best.'

'I thought I did, why choose here? Jesus.'

'Let's look around up here first,' said Grant.

'Purely in the interest of being thorough, of course.' She smiled.

'Of course.' We answered.

Of course there was nothing. Not even dossers. But the myth of the Surgeon probably accounted for that.

'District or Hammersmith and City?' Woodbine enquired.

'Shall we split up?' This was Grant.

'Not fucking likely,' I said. 'Hammersmith and City.'

'Why?' Grant again.

'"Necessity and chance approach not me and what I will is fate."' Woodbine declaimed.

Grant looked impressed. Maybe because she recognised it.

'You public school fuckers are all the same - full of shit.' I said. Because I didn't.

We descended into the underground. The barriers were broken, locked open or locked shut. London Transport just diverted the trains round this stop. Some tube journeys could take up to an hour longer than
they had done. Noise was amplified as we took the steps down. Feral cats, urban foxes, the ubiquitous rats all making up the soundtrack to an unnatural history documentary. The platforms themselves weren't actually underground, they were open to the elements. I never could understand it. Through the entrance, down some stairs, ok, quite a few, but open air at the bottom. You couldn't imagine such a space behind the façade of the tube station and the derelict terraced buildings around it. Go ask Alice.

'Woodbine, you and Grant check the westbound side, I'll do east.'

They nodded and moved away. I shivered. It was cold. I crept down the platform, unsure why I wasn't striding confidently down it. Overturned vending machines had to be negotiated. The seating was unoccupied. At least by anything human. I regretted the commando condition when a cat leapt at me about half way down the platform. At the end of the platform I turned. Heard the first human sound, apart from Woodbine and Grant's profundities, since leaving the car. It was a groan, followed by grunt. It had come from off the end of the platform, a drop of four feet or so; the barriers preventing access had long gone. I looked over. A shape was motionless on the ground among broken bottles and the remains of an office desk. The denim jacket was still in place. I dropped clumsily off the platform edge, nicked a finger on the glass.

'Shit!' I said.

'Careful.' Needles voice was very weak. The denim was stained dark with blood.

'You fall on the glass?'

'No, the blood's from inside the jacket.'

'Let's have a look.'

I went for the buttons. He moved quickly for someone so obviously in pain:

'No. Don't. There isn't much time.'

'Exactly.' But he stopped me again. Gave a wry smile.

'You don't understand. Take my shoe off. Left.'

I humoured him. 'Got it?' he said.

I held up the key.

'PO Box 257, Trafalgar Square. It's the interview tape. Had to lie to the old boy. It'll do the job.'

I went for the denim jacket buttons again. This time he let me. There was no visible wound.

'Where is it?'

'Round the back. It's kidney sized. Don't know why they call him the Surgeon, should be the Butcher.' He coughed.

'How long?'

'Surprised you didn't pass them. Too long, even so.'

'Them?'

'One to carry the refrigerated donor organ container. Ice box to you.'

'It's true then.'

'Oh yes. Unlucky for them.'

'How?'

'I've had the nickname a long time.'

He struggled to push up the sleeve of his jacket. I did it for him. The puncture wounds never really heal.

'I'm HIV. I hope it's for a politician.'

He started to laugh, gave a little cough and finally stopped looking after himself.

Woodbine and Grant reached the foot of the stairs just as I did.

'No luck?'

'For some. I found him. He's dead. Let's go crash at the Safe Room. I'll tell you on the way.'

Back at the Loughborough, there was no room at the inn. The Safe Room was locked and there was no sign of Little Mac and Jackie Carlton. Woodbine was swearing in a mixture of yardie patois and public school slang. I didn't imagine Dreadlocks would be overjoyed at the disappearance of the keys. Grant looked glassy-eyed from fatigue or shock. We got back in the car, I tossed the keys to Woodbine:

'She looks a bit odd. You drive, eh?'

'Where?'

'Can't help you there, I'm afraid.'

I bundled Grant into the back seat, and followed her in. The glassy-eyed look had gone, the tip of her nose was white and there was a vivid spot of colour on each cheek. Her mouth was a tight line.

'Look on the bright side,' I said. 'At least we know they haven't eloped.'

Her mouth twisted a little: 'I think she'd have chosen you for that.'

Woodbine laughed and so did I. She seemed okay now, just her fingers clenching and unclenching on the skirt:

'Careful, I can't guarantee an iron in the next few hours.'

Grant said nothing but stiffly placed her palms flat on her thighs:

'Got any ideas or are you just going to try to be funny?'

'I think you know the answer already. What about you?'

'I'm not feeling particularly humorous, right now.'

Woodbine shot a glance over his shoulder at us:

'Will you two quit the Laurel and Hardy stuff and think of something.'

'Look, Woodbine,' Grant said. 'How about driving while we think?'

'You can be Stan, Grant.' I said, but she ignored me.

Chapter 29

The Commons Bar

Woodbine seemed to be driving generally west. Occasionally detouring for a distant siren or the odd gang with flaming torches. Fires started of course, but mostly they had their burning wood and oil ready for lights out. It helped to be able to see the authorities if you wanted to avoid them after curfew. Two groups clashed outside Waterloo Station, half of it fallen into disuse after Eurostar moved. London Transport declared it unsafe a year after the Olympics, although the Tanzanian shooting team had died when a footbridge collapsed 2 days before the opening ceremony. Woodbine held the car on the clutch for a few minutes. One group was routed; mostly male under 30, white, short haircuts: Pseudo-Nazis, chased off by an eclectic bunch more than half of whom were Asian women. The road cleared and Woodbine floored the accelerator, narrowly missing the last of the Pseudo-Nazis.

'Keep going west,' Grant said.

'Got a plan?' Woodbine asked. Grant grabbed my balls and said:

'Don't say anything, just don't. If I hear one more joke...'

We crossed the river at Waterloo Bridge and turned left towards Whitehall. Woodbine kept going down Whitehall to Parliament Square.

'I'm guessing Parliament next stop,' he said.

'That's right.'

'For what?' I said.

'For a drink, that should please you.'

'What makes you think it's open, much less that they'll let us in?'

'Don't be so negative. I've got a hunch.'

'So's my Auntie Rina, but I never take her advice.'

She just lifted her hand and I held mine palm up: 'Okay, okay. Take a chill pill, would you.'

There were two Praetorians at the entrance to the building. We showed our warrant cards. They looked as blank as statues. Grant 'Smokescreen'-ed them. They were as unmoved as if they'd been carved by Landseer. Grant winked at Woodbine. Both gorillas were male and they were reminded of the fact forcibly by a knee from each of my pals. I was starting to enjoy their company. Woodbine disarmed them and used the guns to render them inoperative for a while. He looked at me doubtfully and gave her one of the Heckler and Kochs after Grant shook her head.

'The Commons Bar.' She said.

In the building itself there were few lights on. There was still a couple of hours to go to Lights Out, but all public buildings had a strict energy saving policy. Even though that horse had fled the country, never mind the stable. We saw a couple of cleaners and the odd politician wandering the gloomy halls. No-one even nodded. We might have been invisible. I could remember when a gun did the opposite. We could hear the racket from the Commons Bar as we turned into the corridor leading to it. It sounded like the Webb Ellis Bar at Twickenham if the Irish had been playing.

We stopped before the door:

'So what's the plan, Wonder Woman?'

'Your part is to have a drink, you can manage that can't you? Just let me do the talking, for once.'

Woodbine shrugged, and I tried to decide what to order as we followed her in.

There was cigarette smoke, I couldn't say I was surprised. Some of the laughter was a little strident; they could have been a theatre audience with a stake in the play. The make-up was trowelled on the women, and some of the men. The Commons looked younger than me when I had first wasted my vote. Or I was just older and they had stayed the same. There were about a hundred or so people in the bar, excluding us. We passed by snatches of conversation on the way to the bar. The guns still failed to draw a second glance. I spotted the Windbag holding forth in front of some of the younger MPs, all male.

We went to the least populated end of the bar. The guy who'd served me during the bar's incarnation as 'Task Force HQ' was once more tossing cocktails and pulling pints for the great and not so good. Grant gave him full beam on the searchlight smile: Little Mac might have had more luck. He sauntered over, eventually. Lifted his chin, 'Get you something?'

'I need a word. In private.' Grant leaned in towards him. 'In the back.'

She appeared unable to help it, even in this most lost of causes.

'There's only me... the bar.'

Woodbine gave him a scary smile: 'I'll do it. I've got experience.'

He gave me the H&K, went to take up his post behind the beer taps. I made as if to follow Grant. She placed a hand on my chest and gave it a push.

'Stay here, have a drink. On the House.' She grinned, pleased at her joke.

I didn't smile back.

Woodbine gave me a Guinness, and slipped into the routine. The blank mask descended on his face once more. The partying continued around me, more dinner partying than Roman orgy. But there was something brittle and desperate about it all the same. Once or twice someone seemed about to approach me for an opinion or some gossip. Without exception they thought better of it and moved away. Soon there was a lacuna in the crowd with a sole occupant, me. It could have been the gun, but I doubted it.

Grant came out, one hand on her gun, the other straightening her skirt, then patting and smoothing her hair. Who was she kidding? I thought. I'd have been a more likely encounter, than the barman. He looked suitably chastened, but had no visible bruises, so I assumed Grant had got what she wanted out of him.

'Well?'

'You'll never guess.' She didn't give me the Megawatts; it was more a dying candle smirk.

'No, I won't.' I took a pull on the Guinness, I'd been making it last.

'The PM was in the freezer for two days, in the back there. The TOD would have been totally fucked up whatever, by the time he'd defrosted.'

'We came here for that? Jesus.'

I finished the Guinness banged the glass extra hard on the bar top. Woodbine looked up sharply, narrowed his eyes at me.

'It's a detail, Murray. And they do matter.' Grant said.

I gave my best faux-English RP: 'To whom exactly?'

'To everyone, Murray. Everyone.'

Woodbine smashed a Guinness down in front of me. I jumped, but it all stayed in the glass.

There was a momentary hush. Jackie Carlton had swept in. Hair coiffed, leopardskin gone. The boxy shoulders of her 80's ish power-suit gave her a military look. She had a look I couldn't quite place, but might have been able to – if I'd known her better. Little Mac was on her heels. That couldn't have been it.

Grant lifted a shoulder, put her neck at an uncomfortable angle:

'Told you I had a hunch.'

I was shaking my head after 'told you'. A bass baritone voice over her shoulder said: 'I don't find that funny.'

It was a former cabinet member. One who'd moved almost seamlessly from Blairite to Brownite. The deep voice had identified her for me immediately. Some had said it would get her the party leadership one day. The same people said the dowager's hump she'd developed had put paid to that. I wondered if she still bothered with the cilice. I hoped to God she wasn't involved in this lot: one mention of Opus Dei and our story's credibility would fly out of the window.

I mouthed 'Fuck off,' at her over Grant's shoulder. She did.

'Well, well, look who's just come in.'

I turned in time to catch Elvis and Jackie Carlton exchanging the barest nod, before he went to buttonhole some other politico.

'What's your brother been up to, though?'

Grant merely shrugged. There wasn't time to answer before Jackie Carlton and Little Mac joined us at the bar.

The woman nodded at me, then Grant. I smelled a heady perfume, more suited to stadia than a smoky bar. I certainly didn't recognise it, she'd not worn it in the previous few days. She cocked her head, and with a brief glance at Grant, said to me:

'Developments?'

'Brownfield sites only, minister.'

'Come on, I'm on your side.'

'Are you?'

Grant spoke to Little Mac: 'Where've you been?'

'She wanted to change, shower and stuff.'

He held up his hands in a what-could-I-do gesture, and waved at the Barman. Woodbine loomed behind the politician, who said: 'Please don't stand behind me. It makes me nervous.'

But I didn't think it did: not nervous, anyway.

Grant went on the offensive: 'All day? I don't think so.'

Jackie Carlton brought herself to speak: 'Grace and favour flat. Sloane Street.'

'Surprised that wasn't being watched.' I said.

'It was after we got there. I stayed outside, for 3 hours.' Little Mac didn't sound impressed.

The former Foreign Secretary gave a smug smile; at the memory of something or other, I supposed.

'Yes well, what do you intend to do?'

At this point Grant turned to me. I had a strange compulsion to shout 'Prompt!' but I'd never known my line, so couldn't be reminded of it.

'The tape.' Grant said.

'Umm, yeah. We think we've got... that is, we think we might... Have something.' It was the best I could do.

'What?' The politico said, naturally enough.

'Not sure yet. We'll know tomorrow.' Grant interrupted:

'We need you to stick with us, at least until we've confronted Uncle... Kilgour.'

'OK, but I want to be there.'

Woodbine asked the question: 'What the fuck are you doing here Ms Carlton? I mean, it's a bit 'the Lion's Den', isn't it?'

'Kilgour's not here, is he?' She didn't look round, just waved airily about.

'What if he had been?' I said.

'But he wasn't, was he?'

'What now?' Little Mac asked.

'Let's get some kip.' Grant replied. 'You go with the Minister, I'm sure she's got somewhere you can go.'

'You go too, Woodbine. Safety in numbers.'

He mimed pulling the neck of a jumper out and looking inside, he smiled. I laughed. They headed for the exit.

'You trust them, Grant?' I looked steadily at her.

'Have to, I s'pose. You?"

'Woodbine I do. Not sure about the other two.' And she nodded as we watched Elvis hesitate a few seconds before following our allies out the door.

'That all you got out of Bartender Bill then?' I was making conversation.

'Like you care.'

She did that pouty thing with her mouth. I liked it. So I said: 'I might, given encouragement.' She laughed and gave her answer: 'In your dreams.'

'Most likely,' I said.

I waved at Bill the Bartender, held up two fingers. He brought me a Guinness and Grant an OJ. A good memory, I liked that in a bartender. 'So, Bartender. Remember all the policemen, before?'

'I remember you, and the fucking ladies' toilets.'

'Hey, that wasn't me, I sent someone in to clean it up.'

He snorted: 'So, what about the coppers?'

'Ever seen any of them, you know. Before the PM...?'

'I saw the high-ranking one before, a few times. With Kilgour. And that other one.'

'Another politico?' Grant said.

'No, a copper. The South African.'

'Namibian,' I said absently.

'Whatever.' He countered.

Grant waved him away and he flounced off to more amenable customers.

'Where are we spending the night, Guv?' Grant said.

'I'll be spending it here, with Bartender Bill. Got any Euros?'

'What for?'

'I'll have to slip him something to keep the bar open if the MP's all fuck off.'

She gave me the eyebrows lift.

'Exactly, I'm not that far down yet: I'd prefer to give him money.'

'Sounds like I'd better stay too. Just in case.'

If I'd been writing the script the Windbag would have been last to leave. He didn't let me down. Although in an alternative version written by him it wouldn't have been on the end of my boot. It was about 5. I took pity on Bill and lay down on a banquette on the opposite side of the room to Grant. Good job I wasn't drunk. Or I'd have...

Chapter 30

A Times from 1982

'Passed out again?'

Grant was trying to keep her distance and shake me awake at the same time. Even I thought I smelled bad. I grunted. She said: 'Shower. I'll get you more clothes from the car.'

She herself had changed to a more practical trouser suit ahead of whatever came our way later. Someone unprofessional would have thought it a pity. So did I. I went into the back behind the bar. Bartender Bill was flat out on the cot. He cocked a sleepy eye at me as I headed for the shower further back.

'No funny ideas, Bill.' I said.

'As if,' he answered.

My self-esteem had taken a battering over the last few days. Served it right.

I'd just stepped out of the steaming shower when Grant came in with my clothes. I could have done without it.

'Comfort not speed, eh?' I didn't like her smile, bright as it was.

'Some people might prefer that. Do you mind?'

She took her time turning: 'Not at all.'

It didn't mean anything. She seemed to me to turn it on for anybody. I was embarrassed and got dressed as quickly as I could. She had walked out front before I'd finished.

We stowed her weapon in the boot and got in the car.

'Trafalgar Square?' I enquired

'William IV Street.' She corrected, and drove smoothly away from the kerb.

The Trafalgar Square Branch of the Post Office wasn't. It wasn't in Traf Square and it wasn't a Post Office in as much no-one actually posted anything there. Anyone lucky enough to have rich relatives outside the UK rented a P.O. Box and hoped illegal euros and cigs were delivered intact. *Post Restante* was the best means of communication between London and anywhere really. It was slow but at least it usually turned up. The pain was the three forms of ID. The national ID card scheme had been scrapped for the third and final time in 2012, when a clerk inadvertently published A-L of the initial 30 million 'applications' on the internet. In his blog. My Space crashed but not until no-one was sure who had copied the information. Most people didn't have a passport after the biometric mark II came in: at 1000 nicker per 3 years it was just too expensive. Besides it was no guarantee of exit from the country. Police and Military were lucky: they all had at least two forms of ID. I had three: if you counted my organ donor card. Naturally, you had to show ID to access the P.O. Box secure area, in spite of the fact you were escorted and you were fucked without a key.

There was no one in but us. It was 10.15. No benefits were paid until midday. The cash would run out about an hour later. The 'postmen' on the door prevented any queuing before 1100. Others inside would eject anyone foolish enough to get in under the pretence of *poste restante* or visiting a box. The 'postman' at the P.O.Box access took his time over the ID check, particularly Grant's – although I didn't remember her breasts actually being on any of the photos. We passed through an airlock, although of course it wouldn't have saved anyone's life in a spaceship. Just the old in one door, and not out the other until it shut behind you. They made me claustrophobic. There was a pneumatic wheeze and we were in. They used to say there were 10,000 boxes at the Traf. There weren't: it just seemed like it because although the numbering wasn't random, after 200 the next block was 5200-5399. This non-system continued until you went mad or you searched all of the boxes there actually were, without finding yours. Unless you got lucky, like we did and the 13th block you looked at was 200-399.

We stood in front of the box. Identical to all the others except for the metal disc with the number 257 etched on it.

'Wonder what's in it?' I said.

'Open the fucking thing and we can go about finding out.' She said.

I patted most of my pockets and looked at Grant. She rolled her eyes. Stamped a foot. I hadn't seen anyone do that since I was 8 years old. I took pity on her and pulled the key out of the first pocket I'd looked in: 'I'm not a complete moron, Grant.'

'No, but you don't miss by much.' She laughed even so.

I opened the box. There was no tape, just Needles' digital recorder. And a very old newspaper, very old indeed. The Times from 1982, just after the troops came home from the Falklands. I took that too.

'Come on, let's go.' I said.

'Where?'

'Jackie Carlton's pad.'

Chapter 31

A Politician in a Bath Towel

We turned into Sloane Street. I told Grant to pull over some 300 yards short of the politician's building's entrance. We parked behind a burned out Bentley. Twoccas, joyriders: there'd been a fad for the last year or so. Twocc it, enjoy it, then bring it back and burn it. Outside the owner's home. It was balls, bravado or just bringing the Law's impotence to its attention. I found it depressing.

Grant turned to me: 'Yeah, now what.'

'I thought we'd listen to Needles' recording out here.'

She seemed about to argue, but subsided into the driver's seat with a sigh. I fumbled with the buttons. Grant snatched the recorder flicked a switch and placed it carefully on the dashboard. Needles voice crossed the void without the aid of table rapping or ectoplasm:

He gave a brief introduction: it was almost like the beginning of an old statement recording.

'Mr Cousins. I'd like to talk to you about the Falklands, Goose Green and 2 Para.'

A mumble made it to the 0s and 1s. It was as intelligible as the binary code.

'Mr Cousins.'

The shout should have melted the binary:

'Yomp you fuckers!'

'Ah, Sgt Major Cousins?'

It had worked just as well for Needles. I could almost hear the click of the former soldier's heels. He gave his name rank and number, and 'sir'-ed Needles up for good measure.

'The Lieutenant sent me, Sar' Major. He wants people to know the truth. It's time, he said.'

I smiled at Needles' own slippery relationship with the truth.

'Are you sure, Sir?' The doubt was audible in the veteran's voice.

'Quite sure, here read this.'

Needles must have shown him something. Or not. The soldier's grasp on reality seemed tenuous at best. Whatever the case, the Sergeant-Major was satisfied.

'Where shall I start, Sir?'

'I want a military report, CSM Cousins. Start with the background, then the detail.

Carry on.'

And he did, it was uncanny. The interview was as real to him as a coin.

'At that time, 1982, I'd been in 3 years. I was waiting for my stripe as we boarded the troop ship. Didn't get it until after the surrender. On the night of May 21st we debouched from the Norland. What a tub! We were first onto the San Carlos beach. It was a relief for about five minutes.

Until the bombing started. The beachhead was established eventually. Early on the 27th the Colonel led the assault on Goose Green. 'H'? Don't make me laugh. Maybe a senior officer or two called him that in the mess at Aldershot. Anyway, before my platoon got anywhere near the objective, we ran across a pocket of Argies. There were ten of them: left behind or deployed forward, depending on your estimation of their courage. *For some reason Captain Grant was with us: great pals, him and our platoon commander, Lieutenant Kilgour. The line kept advancing without us. Grant told Kilgour to sort out the Argies, then rejoin the advance. Grant set off to catch up with the main*

force. Maybe it was an honest mistake.

Grant came running back screaming and swearing, when he heard the shots. There was a massive argy-bargy. It was ridiculous. Two officers pushing and shoving like a playground fight in the middle

of a battle. Grant pulled himself together first. Told Kilgour he'd face justice, friends or no. We left the Argie bodies with their weapons where they'd thrown them, a little too far away to satisfy a war-crimes tribunal.

'Kilgour spent the rest of the 2 day battle trying to stay close to Grant. No matter what it did the the line of advance. Towards the end on the 28th when the line became a string of skirmishes, I lost sight of the rest of our platoon. There was a depression in the terrain. I followed my leader. About 10 yards behind. Grant was about 5 yards in front of Kilgour. He shouted:

'John', I think it was.

He shot him in the face. Never looked back. Didn't know I was there, or didn't care.'

Needles spoke again:

'Did you report this at the time?'

'Of course I did, Sir. Afterwards. By that time the Lieutenant was in despatches, there were rumours of a Military Cross. I was told I was confused. They gave me that fog of war crap: saying I was confused by the adrenalin. I got my stripe the day after I signed a statement to that effect.'

There was a silence. It lasted seconds. Cousins probably filled it with 30 years.

'So he's coming clean. Found God has he? Maybe dying?'

Needles just said: 'thank you Sergeant Major, carry on.'

But he must have waited until he was walking away before he switched the recorder off: a loud, gradually fading voice shouted a warning: 'Incoming!'

Grant's younger sharper eyes caught something a few hundred yards down the street: 'Look, there!' She pointed.

'Where?

It didn't matter, booze and my time of life meant if it was more than fifty yards away the only thing to register was movement.

'Outside Jackie's place. Gone now. Disappeared round the corner.'

'What? A TV crew? Jehovah's Witnesses.'

'A uniform. A police uniform.'

'Anyone you recognise?'

'Not from here,' she said.

The ageing Focus was parked outside the entrance to the grace-and-favour flat. Woodbine and Little Mac were asleep. Grant sighed and rapped the window a little harder than necessary. They had been deeply asleep or they had missed their vocation. The window came down:

'We've been here since we arrived. She told us we'd got to wait outside. Sent the doorman out with a cup of tea.' Woodbine looked tired. Looked at his watch. 'Must have dropped off.'

I exchanged a look with Grant and said :'I think we'll be alright to go in now.'

The flats hadn't exactly been crammed in. Double front four-storey Georgian terrace and only four bells. And a doorman. Politics: nice work, if you can get it. Little Mac pointed at the bell pushes:

'I can't see her name.'

'Let's try this one.' And I pressed a bell marked 'Mrs Wembley.'

Jackie Carlton's voice emerged from the intercom:

'Just wait a few moments. The doorman will see you in.'

The few moments measured 4 minutes. Politician's power play: it was one of Elvis's favourite tricks, summon you to his office and make you wait outside. When you finally got in it was obvious he'd been doing absolutely fuck all while you waited. We piled into the lift. The doorman's palm was still outstretched as the doors closed. I'd felt like spitting in it.

On the way up, I whispered to Grant: 'If I go to the lav, tell her you're desperate too. See if you can snoop around. You can even count her shoes.'

She hesitated, then gave a nod. Little Mac had strained to hear but failed, by the look of him. Woodbine was stony-faced as if our childish whispering was beneath him.

The lift doors opened. The layout was bizarre. Her flat was the 4th floor, all of it. You stepped out into a mini-hotel lobby with vases and an uncomfortable chair, and just one door off it. It looked like expensive wood, real not veneer. The 'IV' on the door was disappointingly tacky: what other number would it be?

The door opened. I'd never seen a politician in a bath towel before.

'I was in the shower.' She said.

But there wasn't a drop of moisture to be seen about her person. She waved an arm at some expensive furniture in the huge lounge:

'Make yourself comfortable, I need to dress.' She went off to her bedroom.

'Always count on those fuckers for the obvious, eh?' I said.

The others sat. I wandered the room having a desultory poke about. Nothing serious. I didn't even look for the key for the locked drawer in the secretoire. Besides, it was antique; if I really wanted a look inside, I could smash it easily. There was a photograph on the wall, not pride-of-place, exactly. I reckoned you could see it from every seat in the room. It showed a very much younger, maybe even more idealistic, Jackie Carlton. I couldn't place the young man with her. He looked familiar. Maybe the clothes were different. The owner of the flat returned as I was peering under a corner of an expensive-looking carpet.

'Put it down carefully, Inspector. That's a kilim. From Persia. Your salary might finance the corner you're holding.' She said, with a sneer.

'You know, I'm absolutely busting. I had to take my mind off it somehow.'

I winked at Grant as I followed Jackie's directions out of the lounge.

When I walked back in, Grant was already out of the room. The other three were sitting in stiff-backed silence. The politician stood up:

'Look, I appreciate you're reluctant to confide...'

'Not at all. As soon as Grant gets back we're going to show you what we've got. Then we'll talk about what we'll do about it.'

She sat down.

'So, what exactly is it?'

Little Mac spoke: 'We think it's enough to...to bring him down.'

She made a show of being shocked: 'What could it be?'

As an actor she made a good politician. But I thought she should have been better. I felt my hands slipping on the wheel and the metaphorical car beginning to skid. Grant came in: mouthed 'Sixty two' over the others' heads. I stifled a laugh. We played the recording to them: I watched the woman, Grant watched her brother. The politician went for a poker face, out of the corner of my eye I caught a look of shock on Little Mac's face. Woodbine just gave a bitter laugh as the recording ended.

Jackie Carlton crossed her legs and tapped her re-manicured fingers on the chair arm: 'So, we'll confront him, is that the idea?'

'Pretty much.' I said.

'This recording is the only proof? Where's the reporter?'

'He took the ferry, to the other side.' I said.

'France?' She said, puzzled. 'He's safe enough there. Will he spike the story if we tell him to? That might be the price of Kilgour's resignation.'

'I don't think it'll be a problem.'

'How do we do it?' But she was thinking out loud.

Little Mac said: 'We'll bring him here. I'll call him.'

My head jerked round at that, but I said nothing. Our hostess was speaking again: 'I think I should do it, minister to minister, he'll come for me.'

'I expect he'll come for his son, too.' I said.

Little Mac looked sick, glanced at his sister. Grant's face was like polished stone. Woodbine picked at his teeth and examined his fingernails. The politician seemed to be fighting a smile, as if she'd reached for a bow and found a bazooka. I wondered exactly how much she knew about Macaulay Kilgour.

I looked at Woodbine: 'We need a favour. Can you get the stuff from the safe-room? The SmartDisks, the cassette tape, the Webley. And my copies of the reports. Can you do it in under an hour?'

'Getting me out of the way?' he said.

'No, get back in an hour and you can watch the final reel.'

Little Mac tossed him two bunches of keys. Woodbine looked over at the politician and said: 'I'll let myself out.'

A sleek looking telephone handset rang about an hour later. The ministerial fingernail pressed a button and 'Kilgour' came forcefully over the speaker. The fingernail pressed a 3 digit combination and Jackie Carlton said:

'Just push the door. You know the way.'

I thought of expressing my opinion of her. It was doubtful whether even those particular four letters would have dented her composure in the slightest. She got up to let Kilgour in. My first instinct was to laugh: it was a very smart uniform, the boots were shiny. It looked as though he'd awarded himself all the medals he would have had, if he'd stayed in the army. Grant managed not to look like a bad porn star when the plumber arrives near the start of the film, Little Mac was finding it harder. The only other person in the room immune to 'the charisma' was Jackie Carlton. But then she was used to transmitting, not receiving.

'Sit down, Minister.' She said.

He did: 'Little Mac, what's this about, son?' he said.

'Don't call me that.' Little Mac said.

'Shall we begin?' Jackie wanted to get on. Sniffing the blood on the fox.

'We'll give him another half-an-hour.' I held up my hand to stop the arguments.

'Nice Uniform, Mac. I preferred the lounge suit. More man of the people, eh?'

Kilgour didn't rise to it. Or maybe he judged the other players in the game as more important. Carlton's fingers drummed on the expensive fabric of her chair. Grant sat stiff as though the slightest movement would cause her to shatter like a spun sugar sculpture. Little Mac was wriggling like a strung-out speed freak. I thought better of suggesting a game of 'Happy Families.' Mr Strong the Dictator leapt to his feet and began pacing about the room. I could see the sooty mark where his mascara had smudged. Image was all. Or everything was image. I didn't know which.

The handset cracked the brittle silence. The fingers allowed the talking once more and Woodbine was soon in the room. It seemed smaller after his arrival and the imminent resolution of the matter. I tossed Grant the digital recorder: I was just too miserable, and not drunk enough, to play Poirot in the last chapter. Besides, she'd done most of the work; I'd been along for the ride and the view.

'You might like to listen to this, Uncle Mac.'

Grant's eyes had the glassy look of a doll's and she pushed the button. Everyone listened in silence. At the end, I swear Kilgour ducked as he heard Cousins shout 'Incoming!' To his credit, there was no bluster. He simply said,

'I see.'

Jackie Carlton allowed herself the faintest smirk, before composing herself:

'Resignation. That's all. In the House, tomorrow. Live TV everything.'

'Of course, whatever's required.'

I found myself looking for a puddle on the expensive kilim, the charisma had leaked out so suddenly.

It felt like a titanic anti-climax, until Little Mac pulled out a gun.

Chapter 32

Like I Was Speaking Esperanto

'We'll be leaving now, Uncle Mac.' He said. The gun was already at the Leader's back. Kilgour's face was twisting, grimacing like a Bedlam lunatic's: not a word came out of his mouth. I wasn't interested. Grant looked simple, her jaw slack as a drunk's. Woodbine's face was expressionless: he made no move to his gun. Jackie Carlton's face registered surprise, of course. But there was something else too: a calculating look - as if she was working out how to turn this new development to her advantage.

'I'll take the Focus: don't try to follow us. He'll be driving, but not for long if you do.'

Little Mac dug the pistol in Kilgour's back for emphasis. The Leader had not said a word. They left. I looked for a window with a prospect on the street. Kilgour strolled round to the driver's side: the gun was nowhere in sight. Carlton picked up the handset, fingernailed the speaker off, then hit a speed-dial.

'Endgame.' Was all she said, before hanging up.

'Are you sure?' I asked her. 'I think we've been castled.'

Woodbine, Grant and I stood outside on the street: the woman in the flat had ordered us out, flexing the muscles of command. I shook Woodbine's hand: 'What will you do?'

'My sister's got a plan. It's our pension plan, but Barclays don't know about it. Call me, if you want anything.'

I watched his back recede down the street. Grant was quiet, I didn't like that: 'That's it then, hey?' A damp squib.'

'I don't even know what that is. But it's not over, not yet.'

'Why?'

'Loose ends.'

'There are always loose ends. People don't notice. Not really.'

'You should know better than that.' She looked at something at the far end of the street, or the far side of the moon.

'Well, I need a drink, I do know that. Before I make peace at the nick.'

She looked at me like I was speaking Esperanto: 'Don't you think your boats and bridges are burned?'

'I'm a good swimmer. Don't forget McCrackers' gun. They won't do anything. They might even invite us for a drink to celebrate you joining CID.'

'You really think so?'

'No, I don't. But I'd like them to feel ashamed for not doing it, come on.'

We piled into the unmarked and headed for our nick.

Gina Gina was on the desk. No Jerry Patel. He was due some time off. I'd get him into CID if I could; it was the least I could do.

'When's Jerry on next?' I braced myself for the double-talk answer.

'On sick leave, on sick leave. Indefinite, Guv. Indefinite.'

I didn't want to ask: 'What happened?'

Gina's mouth opened then closed. Twice, as she looked over my shoulder.

'Kaffir in the wrong place at the wrong time. Some trouble at his parents in the Enclave. These things happen.' Fritz the Twat's grin made the acid rise with the anger, but Grant held my arm.

'You be very careful, Murray. Nigger, Nigger-lover makes no difference to me. Or to a lot of others, I think you'll find.' Fritz sneered.

The shock on the others' faces was understandable; he must have been very sure of himself to say the N-word in public. Anyone could have walked in off the street.

Anyone hadn't: Elvis had, followed by his driver, Joyous Wilson. The remark hadn't been heard, or it was ignored. Elvis said: 'Meeting CID 15 minutes. All three of you.'

As Fritz set off to follow at his master's heel I caught his foot with my toe and gave it the playground flip. He nearly broke his neck trying not to knock Elvis over. Wilson caught him before he went all the way down, she was grinning: 'Watch your step, Sarge. There isn't always someone willing to help out.'

I wondered if she was a Christian: I know my estranged-wife would have kicked him on the way down, and I wished I'd thought of it.

The ex-Task Force in its entirety was in CID: Fritz, myself, Grant, Off-Cut, the rest. And Ari Chryssipous. Elvis strode in: 'You're it. We have a manhunt: we need co-ordination and we need it from here. Chryssipous, you're in charge.'

'Who are we looking for?' I asked.

'Former leader of the Tony Party, Macaulay Kilgour and his nephew, Macaulay Grant.' He said it slowly, as if he was trying hard not to shout. He looked at me closely for a moment: 'Your talents may be better used on the ground, perhaps.' He turned on his heel and left.

'Loose ends.' I said to Grant.

Ari came and put an arm round my shoulders. I shook it off, drunk as we'd been together in the past, we'd never once had that slurred, emotional 'yermabestpal' moment. Why start now? I thought.

He straightened up: 'A word, in private.'

He flicked a glance at Grant, who brushed the back of her hand along her uptilted chin and into his face. I thought Ari should watch out for the ulcer. Holding that much bile in was bound to be bad for his digestion.

We were over by the window: the tower blocks loomed out of the mist like the superstructure of a battleship; a Foggy Day in London Town. Maybe Ari's proximity would always have that effect on me. We'd played the daft association game for so long. People changed, maybe it was time I did. He rubbed the side of his nose with a forefinger, I thought it was a tic, he didn't seem to know he was doing it:

'Umm, you need to make sure you're on the right team at the final whistle, Ray. I have. You'd better, if you want to get out, see Yol-'

'I don't as a matter of fact. And as for being on the right team? Surely the game doesn't finish 'til they blow that whistle. What if Supersub comes on and scores twice in the last minute, eh? Or are we playing an Italian league match?'

'You were always such a smartarse, Ray.'

'They're the best kind, Ari. No-one tries to lick them.'

'Stick around for the briefing, it'll be 5 minutes. Then fuck off, fuck off until it's all over. This manhunt's no job for smartarses.'

'You know what happens sometimes, in a hunt, Ari?'

'Educate the Greek, why don't you?'

'Sometimes a hound gets injured, they die better than the fox, but dead's dead. No cunt on a horse gives a fuck about anything on the ground, Ari.'

'Well, efharisto poli, Ray. Efharisto poli.'

'You're welcome,' I said, and walked over to stand with Grant for the briefing.

'Ports and Airports are closed to the fugitives, the Border Guards have been issued with photographs and a description of the vehicle...'

It all turned to blah, as I marvelled at the efficiency of it all: as if all the parts had been written and the props put in place before we'd made our entrance.

'...A source close to the fugitives has suggested they may make for Westminster, the Mall and its environs. I propose that DI Murray, DS Du Toit, and P- ahem – DC Grant patrol the area.'

I winked at Grant:

'One car, how many square miles is that?'

'We're expecting a ransom demand.' Ari's face reddened.

'Why?'

'Information received.' He just managed not to stutter.

Grant and I exchanged a look, asking ourselves, 'from whom?'

I crooked a finger at Fritz, who looked less than happy, although he gave Grant an appreciative look. We left the building.

It was 7.15, there was a London peculiar made all the more special by the petroleum product substitutes people found to use. It seemed to me nowadays that the slightest hint of fog or mist deep-fried the whole of the city. A good Glasgow boy like me should have felt at home, and truth to tell, I did. Fritz made a face as I told him to get in the back Grant shot me a look of thanks:

'Are we really going to drive all around the area on the off chance of spotting them? That's mad.' She said.

'Not if I can help it, we won't. I need a drink. I might manage without a smoke and I reckon we might as well watch the TV for a bit.'

'I know a place,' Fritz offered.

'Glad you know something,' I laughed.

'128, Piccadilly, Grant.'

She held up a hand over her shoulder, middle finger extended. She'd heard him.

It sounded familiar. The address; it was still a good one, more or less. Mayfair and Piccadilly weren't what they were, but then, where was?

The building was quite imposing, some lawn had become urban jungle sometime in the last ten years, the building itself was a block of Victoriana bearing the scars of true neglect. The gates and railings had long gone, stolen and sold to a scrapyard. I recognised it now, I'd once attended a military police liaison conference there, when such things happened - never mind mattered. It was the Royal Air Force Club: or it had been. We parked the car, it blended in well with the others strewn like a child's toys on the grass-cracked concrete. A brass-plate no longer proudly announced the RAF Officer's home from home: a Perspex-covered hastily stencilled piece of card read:

'Southern African Expatriates Club.'

Fritz barged past, used the bell pull. It worked, surprisingly. It wasn't the last surprise. The door was answered by a woman of about 30, far eastern Asian in appearance. Fritz showed a card: I couldn't read it, the woman could.

'Password.' I rolled my eyes at Grant. More infantile games.

'Voortrekker.' Du Toit said with a straight face. I stifled a giggle as the woman showed us in.

It was a cliché: the faded splendour of a National Trust building. Brighter, or just darker, patches of wallpaper where any good art had been sold, stored or simply stolen. The pictures that remained were portraits of dress-uniform dummies, who were probably somewhat more portly and florid in real life. If you counted the military as any kind of real life, that is. The furniture was antique and in need of restoration for the most part. We followed the woman down the hall. Fritz leered all the way.

We went into something called the Corday room. It was where the long ago conference had been held. There was a TV in the corner, beside a guerilla bar; cans, fridges, bottles and crumpled notes in an ice-bucket on the bar. The woman stood behind it; the three or four middle-aged males clamoured for refills, although it would have been easy enough to help themselves in her absence. She got to us:

'Gentlemen, Miss?'

'Got any Guinness?' I said. She opened a fridge and threw a can over her shoulder. I caught it. A bigger shock for me than the other two. The woman was still at the fridge:

'Well?'

'Lion Beer.' The woman repeated the trick. Fritz half fumbled the catch.

'I'll have a coke, please.' Grant said.

The woman plucked a bottle from the fridge and placed the kewpie bottle gently on the bar top. I let Fritz pay.

'There's the TV, Murray, happy now?' He said.

Chapter 33

At The Cenotaph

The TV was a model that would have been 20 years old the last time I'd been in the building. A Ferguson: British made. If you could call assembling Japanese and Korean built components making. I'd forgotten how blurred these steam driven sets made the pictures. Had we really not noticed that, when these were the cutting edge of video technology? There was a programme on recycling cooking oil for fuel showing.

'What is this dump, Fritz?' I asked.

'You saw the sign.'

'Not very popular though, is it?' I looked round at the rest of the clientele.

'Busier at meetings,' he grunted.

'Really?' Grant raised an eyebrow.

'There were 200 at the last rally...' he stopped.

'Rally?' I raised my eyebrow.

'Stop it!' Grant said. I didn't fancy another squeeze of my lovenuts, so I did.

'What kind of rally, Fritz?' Grant prodded.

'You know, not political exactly, just...'

'Yeah, just...' and I turned to the TV, fascinated by the connection between my last fish supper and the smell of the city.

I finished my drink. Knocked a fist on the bar for attention. The woman gave me a look to melt my giblets: she leaned to the side and down, remaining perched on a high stool. Without looking she snagged a Guinness can and tossed it in one movement. I caught it; somewhat less elegantly than last time. Fritz let out a snigger. It was a mystery to me how Fritz and his ardent meeting goers put up with this. Maybe she was some kind of court jester figure; maybe they 'put her in her place' from time to time. I tapped the top of the can before opening it. I covered the wedge-shaped hole in the top with my mouth pretty rapidly, just in case. The woman behind the bar nodded and gave a grudging smile.

'Fritz, did we come here for any particular reason?' I did wonder.

'Nah, it's in the area.'

But he had been looking at the door to the Corday Room off and on since we came in.

Grant had been quiet.

'Penny for yours.' I said.

'Considering what they're worth, I'll take it.' Her smile almost made it to her eyes.

'What? Or who?' I asked.

'Later.' She darted a look at Fritz, who was trying to look up the skirt of the woman on the stool behind the bar. From the flat face she gave him you'd never have known she'd caught him. Only from the whitening of the knuckles on her spritzer glass.

A news flash was announced:

'Live to Whitehall now. An incident is unfolding at the Cenotaph...'

The picture cut to Flabby Flak Jacket. Didn't anyone else work at the BBC? The Cenotaph stood distantly solemn in the background: it was strange to see it without the marchers streaming past. Two figures were on the plinth, next to the weakly fluttering flags. The reporter finished his preamble:

'A hostage situation has developed at the War Memorial. Viewers may remember two years ago when a former serviceman was shot at the monument during a protest against the suspension of military pensions. At the time police believed he was carrying an explosive vest.'

But he hadn't been, he'd been on the streets for a few years before mounting his protest; the law of clothing layers had applied.

'Police have not yet arrived on the scene but your reporter called 999 a few moments ago on arrival here at The Cenotaph. The public are advised to keep clear.'

Flabby Flak Jacket knew his business: that would ensure a crowd of gawpers, gawkers and ghouls for the drama playing out on camera.

'No explosives are visible, but we believe the younger of the two men is armed. Now back to the studio...'

'Let's go Fritz, Grant. They're playing our song.'

'And what song is that?' they both said.

'I reckon it's Two Little Boys.' And they looked as blank as my list of ideas about what to do when we got there.

We pulled up in Whitehall. First on the scene. Apart from the BBC, of course. I wondered who had called them. The crowd had started to gather. No-one had dared go nearer than 50 metres; thereby proving the public's ignorance of security guidelines. If we'd had any kind of manpower, we'd have set up a cordon 250 metres from the suspected bomber. Since there were three of us, I told Fritz to keep people back as best he could, perhaps by putting the wind up the BBC guy.

He smiled and looked as though he'd enjoy that.

'You know it's them, don't you?' Grant said to me.

'Who else would it be?' I said.

'What were you thinking about, before?'

'Why now, who put him up to it? It's just not Little Mac.'

'It looks like him.'

'Don't be a prat, Ray. You know what I mean.'

'Let's find out what he means.'

We were about 20 metres away. Little Mac had got some cuffs from somewhere. Kilgour was wearing them. The gun was still in evidence, but I doubted there was a bomb. I held up both arms, palms forward. Grant put hers on her head, out of respect to the military location, maybe.

'Hey! Macaulay!' Childish, I knew. They looked over. Little Mac said: 'Stop! Stop there!' The gun was pointing at us now, wavering, as though he found it unbearably heavy.

'Let us come up, we can talk about it.' What, I didn't know. It was a line from TJ Hooker or something.

Grant spoke: 'Hey, bro! What a mess, eh?'

He shook his head: 'I'm cleaning it up. It's my mess.'

'Don't do anything stupid, Little Mac.'

'Shut up!' His sister hissed at me.

'Come on, bro. The drunk is right for once. Don't do anything stupid.'

Little Mac looked hopped up. It was a cold, foggy day, like I said. The boy was sweating. He licked his lips.

'Can you get the BBC crew to come up?'

'What for?' I said. Grant gave me a not quite murderous look: I could have done it for assault with a deadly though.

'For him.' He nodded at his 'Uncle', Father-figure, lover, whatever he was. The politician in question was mouthing words: practising his speech to the camera. It had better be good, it would be his last one way or the other.

'You want me to go?' I said to Grant.

'Yeah, I'll keep the lid on it here.'

Flabby Flak Jacket looked doubtful. I grabbed a handful of the canvas holding his kevlar and gave him full power alcohol: 'What are you worried about? You're dressed for it. More than I am.'

I let him go. He stumbled, recovered and barked out orders at his crew of camera- and sound-man. Kick the dog. I turned and assumed they'd follow. They did. So did Fritz. I pondered again if he'd been sent to keep an eye on us, or him out of the way.

Little Mac appeared to be in control of the situation: he called out to Flabby Flak Jacket: 'Bosanquet! Mr Kilgour has a statement to read out. Record it, do it live, whatever: we don't care.'

The OB van was still fifty metres away: they were taking a chance on wireless technology by the look. Or perhaps there was no intention of going live.

The BBC reporter got dangerously close to the two Macs, cued up his team and gave the introductory spiel. The boom mike was at the sound man's shoulder like an anti-tank gun. It wasn't going to stop the juggernaut. I was mystified as to what the ex-pol was going to say. He gave his speech with his hands cuffed behind him:

'Fellow citizens,' he began, and I prepared for a mental game of bullshit bingo and hoped I had enough capacity to count the clichés:

'It has been a time of strain for all of us: our visionary leader taken from us at his moment of destiny...'

A euphemism I'd never heard before.

'I myself wished to take the reins and recreate the greatness of Britain with the electorate's help. I am but a man, with faults, I realise now that I cannot lead as you would wish to be led.'

I whispered to Grant:

'What a load of cock!'

She eyed me through slits:

'If you only knew.'

Kilgour was still pontificating: as far as I could tell he'd said nothing of import; incriminating or exculpatory. He seemed to be winding up; the flecks of foam on his lips belying the bland, clichéd oratory emerging from them. He stopped, waiting for applause: the gawpers were silent. This wasn't what they'd come to see.

Little Mac jabbed the gun in his ribs:

'Tell them, tell them what you did!'

'I made sure a potential leader became one, that's all.'

'TEELLLLLL THHEEEMMMMM!'

The crowd perked up, this was more like it.

Kilgour looked sadly at Little Mac:

'It's not as if he was your father, is it?'

And I saw then how sick the man was. I looked at Grant, whose face showed the conflict of 20 years and the knowledge of evil, shame and love in equal proportions.

Then Little Mac shot him, in the face. Twice, before he blew his own off with a further two. My hand fell away from Grant's arm as she ran to her brother.

An ambulance and several cars arrived: too late as was often the case. The usual suspects arrived on the scene: Ari, Off-Cut, a few uniforms. It would be a matter of crowd-control; that was all. The cameras were still rolling: so Ari put himself in close-up and made a statement:

'This is a crime scene: can I ask you to stop filming? There'll be a fuller statement later. Thanks.'

It was a mystery where Ari had acquired all those media skills: maybe the greasy pole held an attraction for him after all. It would be interesting to see what he'd have to do to live down being my partner for so long. He buttonholed me:

'I'll be taking over Ray. You being a witness and all.'

'Sure. Go steady: that's her family over there. What's left of it.'

I punched the cameraman. His camera was still rolling: getting a close-up of the obscenity that was two former soldiers' blood on a monument to others' spilled elsewhere. Off-Cut tried to pull me away: he was easy to shake off. I took a seat on the kerb and held my head in my hands.

Chapter 34

Endgame

Back at the nick. I made a statement. Grant made a mess of a fingernail. Two uniforms had had to drag her away from her brother's corpse. She sat on the tubular steel and plastic chair, rocking, uttering not a word. I walked over; put a hand on her shoulder:

'They're going to want a statement.' She looked up, dull-eyed:

'They can write it themselves, wouldn't be unusual.'

'It wouldn't, at that.'

I looked over at the fire doors swinging. Elvis had entered the building; he clapped his hands together:

'Let's see if we can tidy this up, J-ahem- the Prime Minister pro-tem wants me to report directly to her.'

'Right back to where we started from, eh?'

Elvis swallowed. It looked like it hadn't been anything tasty.

'Murray. Yes. Made your statement?'

'Of course, sir. Only, I don't think Grant's capable of...'

'I'll do it now.' And she waved an arm at Ari and walked over to his desk.

'Judgement as good as ever, Murray.' Elvis said.

At Ari's desk, I said to Grant: 'I'll be outside in the car.'

It was boring in the car. I rooted about in the side-pocket on the passenger side. A packet of spearmint, a leaky biro, a bent paper clip and an old 1 GB memory stick. I shoved it in the illegally mounted stereo. We all had them put into the official cars. The police radio hardly ever worked. A song by a turn of the century band came on: stupid name. Something about monkeys. Good song though, a title for our times more than theirs: 'Everything's Average Nowadays.'

The song cut out at the last chorus. A familiar voice came out of the speakers:

'Call me Jackie...' There was a non-commital grunt. The politico continued: 'You know what they'll find, don't you? You know what he is.'

'What?'

'A monster. You'll admit that. He cannot be allowed to lead the country, a man like that...'

Another grunt.

'That soldier will say he killed your father.'

'Say.' Little Mac said.

'Well, let's just say there are no real secrets in Whitehall or Westminster. A terrible thing, what he did.'

'Terrible.' Echoed Little Mac: the word described the pain in his voice. There followed the radio producer's nightmare; seconds of dead air. I wondered how he'd made the recording without Jackie Carlton's knowledge. The next song was very old indeed: the Boomtown Rats, Looking After #1. I turned Bob off, it was an odd song for a charity fiend to sing.

Grant came out. I got out, took the driver's seat. She sat in the passenger side:

'I didn't think you had a licence.'

'I haven't. Not any more.'

'You can't drive!'

'It's like riding a bike. Put your seatbelt on.'

'Where are we going?

'I'll just drive. See where we end up, how's that?'

'Not out.' She said, and she leaned back and the corners of her mouth twitched upward for a second, before she shut her eyes.

I pulled up at Waterloo Pier. We both got out of the car. I walked out to the jetty. Mimed a discus throw. She looked at me steadily. I looked back: 'What did you throw in?'

'It was a laptop.'

'Yours?'

'Yes.'

'What did you know about Smokescreen?'

'Just enough to make things turn out for us.'

'Us?'

'Little Mac and I.'

'Who was behind Smokescreen?'

'Mac Kilgour, obviously.'

'Obviously.' But I didn't really think so. 'And both Macs dead is a result then?' It was a cruel thing to ask.

'Of course not. But we didn't know what was on the recording.'

'Did you discuss the recording with Little Mac?'

'No, how could I?'

'He knew what was on it, though.' Her eyes widened: 'Don't be ridiculous!'

'He did though. Jackie Carlton told him.'

'Did you know there was a secret? About 'Uncle Mac'? No, don't bother, of course you did. That was the whole point.'

'It was about ruining him politically. It's all that would have mattered to him.'

'And the Cenotaph business?'

'Little Mac. None of that was in the plan, before.'

'Kilgour didn't make the statement you wanted, did he? Why shoot him?'

'Come on, you heard what he said.'

'Yes. Yes, I did.' I put a hand on her arm, but she turned away and walked back to the car. I wished I didn't live in a no-smoking country.

In the car, I told her: 'Look, I don't care. It doesn't matter.'

'About Smokescreen?'

'That too.'

'I'm glad. I'd leave if I could.'

'Maybe we'll be able to, one day.'

The story ended pretty much the same anyhow. Tragic loss of another statesman. Little Mac's suicide a result of post-traumatic stress, what else? Jackie Carlton called a general election. There were no police escorts; a policy reverse announced by the new Chief of the Met, Elvis Pressley. The turn out was some 60%. She won. We rejoined the EU, the St Pancras and Paddington links opened. The trains ran to what were inevitably called emigration camps, or reverse Sangattes. Processing centres to enable the EU to cope with the flood out of the UK. Grant and I applied for our number to go.

Epilogue

One year later.

About five hundred people stood queueing on the platform at St. Pancras for one of the 'Special Trains' to Dover. Grant and I were among them. We wanted to take the ferry, rather than fly out of Heathrow. The queue moved slowly. Families, singletons, children, some senior citizens; all talking, excited but apprehensive. It was a sunny, bitterly cold day. There were so many bags, cases, trunks: all manner of portable goods. One older guy was carrying a crystal chandelier. At the front of the queue were unsmiling border guards and a chain-link fence. Just before the turnstile, you surrendered your possessions to a chirpy functionary in a quasi-uniform. He gave

the people at ticket for each item and an assurance that he would attend to their safekeeping personally. People got quieter the nearer they got to the front, awed by the leap into the unknown, perhaps.

There were 15 or so in front of us. I turned to Grant:

'I can't do it.'

'What?'

'I'm not going. I couldn't go with Yol and I can't go with you, I'm sorry.'

'You're really going to stay in...in this!'

'I can't explain.'

She snatched her arm from mine. Began moving more forcefully toward the front of the queue.

'Wait,' I shouted after her. She didn't look back. I jostled a few angry people to catch her up. She continued to ignore me. She was at the turnstile.

'Papers!' The border guard barked at her.

She handed him a passport and passed over to the other side.

'You!' The same guard snarled at me. 'Travelling, or not?'

'No, no I'm not.'

He leaned close: 'Well fuck off out the way then!'

I watched through the chain link fence as she disappeared into the Special Train. I'd been waiting for a wave, a look, something. I was disappointed. Some time later the platform was clear. There was no-one around at all, except for me, and an old woman. Quite erect, bright, bright eyed. She might have been someone's Grandmother left behind by mistake. She waved me over:

'You could not go either?' I shook my head. She went on:

'You will think me silly. I could not get on the train.'

There was something central European in the cadence, the faintest trace of consonant confusion.

'No, I could not. It was the name you see. 'Special Train'.'

'What do you mean?' I asked.

'I travelled on one before, with my mother and father, I was 10 years old. It was written on the side of the train. Sonderzug.'

She shook her head and walked away. But I didn't see her. I saw a smokescreen slowly clearing and a woman stepping out into the light:

'Call me Jackie...' she said.